I0536978

Ancient Danger

Mata Hari Series, Book #3

Jo-Ann Carson

Praise for

The Mata Hari Series

Book 1 – Covert Danger

*****5 Star Reviews *****

"LOVE it!
I so loved this story! It was like someone FINALLY made James Bond a female.....only mad her better and badder! It was great to be able to read about a strong woman, but who isn't afraid to walk on the wild side with Sebastian! The chemistry between Sadie and Sebastian is so hot, it jumps off the pages at you. I could not put this book down... Sadie has many sides to her like a beautiful faceted jewel and I loved reading about all of them. The locations she visits made me feel like I was with her on her jet setting adventures. This would be a book to not only add to your TBR pile, but keep it and re-read it from time to time. (Gerianne Slavinsky, April 7, 2015, Amazon and Goodreads)

"Brave, intelligent, beautiful and witty - Sadie Stewart seems to be unbeatable in this face-paced suspense series. But like every great spy adventure the bad guys are just as cunning and complex as the good guys. Nothing, and no one, is black and white in this story. Not the sexy Dutch art dealer, the mysterious Egyptian arms dealer, the father-figure CIA handler, or Sadie herself. Add this compelling cast of characters to boat chases, fashion shoots, sumptuous palace rendezvous and museum heists set in Venice, Amsterdam, Cairo and New York and you've got an adventure to be remembered." (JReads, April 4, 2015, Amazon)

"A great heroine, great hero and an evil villain who manages to exude sex appeal and charisma. A model by day and spy by night, Sadie Stewart races around Italy, Holland, Egypt and NY as she tries to stop a major heist at the Metropolitan Museum. I read it in one day and can't wait to read the next book in this series." (Must Love Books, April 3, 2015, Amazon)

"... a wild, suspenseful ride. Complex plot, great characters, danger. This book has it all...Each time I thought things couldn't get worse for the heroine, the author ratchets up the stakes...Did I say the heat was intense? Oh, yes!" Marsha R West, Amazon, April 6, 2015
"... wonderful, romantic sexy romp which takes you from the canals of Venice to the quaint streets of old Amsterdam, a palace in Cairo and then to New York city. With complex characters and steamy love scenes..." (Helena Korin, Amazon, April 2015)

"An all action spy story... A grand adventure through the art world and mystic ancient Egyptian artifacts. Amsterdam to Cairo to New York. Fun and frolics, smiles and stilettoes, sex and friendship. It's all here. Great fun." (Petula Winmill, Amazon, April 1, 2015)

Copyright Page

©2015 Jo-Ann Terpstra
ISBN – 978-0-9738902-5-9

Cover design by Nina French

Dedicated to:

My beautiful daughters,

Hannah and Jasmin

who are the magic in my world.

CHAPTER 1

Venice, Italy
October

*S*tifling *the* *desire* to scream, Sadie stood on top of the fourteenth-century Venetian palazzo looking out over the lagoon and its islands. No point risking the lives of others. She took a deep breath of the salty air blowing in off the Adriatic Sea. The red-tiled rooftops, round domes and cathedral spires of the ancient city spread to the west. For hundreds of years noblemen had used this perch to watch the arrival of merchant ships from the Orient with their exotic wares. Now it had become her trap.

Below, an opera singer in the bow of a gondola serenaded young lovers nestled inside, while the gondolier at the stern in his blue and white striped shirt navigated the still night waters. Venice, a city steeped in history and secrets, a place where anything could happen in a heartbeat and did; a sanctuary for people like her who wanted to disappear. It was her second home.

Happy sounds of the party roared around her, while her heart stilled. Sadie kept her cover-girl smile in place, as a tingle crawled across her scalp. Why tonight of all nights?

She'd been with Sebastian for six months, not always in the same geographical location, but together-together in the way that really counts—in the heart. Tonight was their six month anniversary and she'd wanted everything to be perfect. That's why she'd chosen to meet him in Venice.

The fact that a big masquerade ball had been planned for a charity they both supported made it all the more perfect. She looked around, taking in the success of the event with her eyes and the danger with her mind.

Who could recognize her? A black lace mask fashioned by a local artist covered the top half of her face. She'd dressed in a red, silk and satin Marie Antoinette gown that hid her model thin stature. She blended well with the reveling crowds that packed the Restaurant terrazza.

Inside, a band dressed in embroidered gold knickers and topcoats played modern dance music heavy on the sax. Their sultry music set a provocative tone. The smell of expensive perfumes and the sweat of people hungry for excitement saturated the warm night air with a growing sense of anticipation that had a throbbing pulse of its own.

Curling a loose tendril of her long red hair around her index finger, Sadie studied the moment, slowing it down, soaking in every detail. What had she been thinking, leaving herself so exposed? Had she been thinking? She swallowed.

Fifteen yards to her left loomed the predatory male. Closing in.

Watching him from the corner of her eye for the last ten minutes she'd assessed the threat level. Way too high for her liking. Tall, lean and sturdy like a basketball center, the man had a fluid and menacing air about him as if he readied for battle. He wore a black woolen cape over black clothes, a tricorne hat over a white wig and a gold, baroque, satiro mask. It was the popular carnivale guise of the satyr, a creature from Greek mythology known for reveling in the pleasures of the flesh and it covered the man's identity well, but not his intent.

He looked at her as if she had a bulls-eye on her forehead, and the way he moved, stealth-like, hunting his prey, set off her warning bells. The hair on the nape of her neck rose. He could be an assassin sent to kill her to make her secrets disappear, or he could be someone from her past wanting revenge in a more personal way. Given her former life as a spy, many possibilities came to mind. She balled her fists, letting the sharp edges of her nails pierce her skin.

She searched for his hands, but they were hidden beneath his long, black cloak. Did he have a weapon? Her senses sharpened as she scanned the area again. He appeared to be alone.

Two couples close to her chatted about the fruity bouquet of their wine. One tasted an edge of oak, another chocolate. Not a friend in sight. Pulling up her heavy skirt, she prepared to move if he came closer. In peak condition she could run fast, but her gown and stupid shoes would slow her down.

Perhaps enough to get caught this time. And then what?

The satyr took another step towards her and they made eye contact for the first time. A cold connection zapped between them, like the kiss of a lizard. Sweat trickled down the back of her neck and she shivered.

Escape. She had to escape. People flooded the terrace and restaurant inside, like a tightly knit school of piranha. She could barely breathe let alone move, the place was so packed. Where were the security men? She'd insisted they hire an extra team of trained people, because there would be so many wealthy people attending. Big money draws crime. Had they been distracted? Distracted professionals—that was never a good sign. She licked her lips and edged away from her hunter.

If only she could slip into the shadows. But there were none. Exposed and vulnerable. She couldn't scream for help, because that would force the stalker to make a move. That could get nasty. Squeezing her fists more tightly she waited for her moment, knowing that choosing it wisely could be a matter of life or death.

So many people—innocent people. She couldn't let anyone get hurt. Not because of her, and the choices she'd made in her life. As her pulse quickened, the irony of the situation humored her. She had suggested this site for the charity ball, because it looked like an enchanted palace in a storybook, and they were raising money for childhood cancer research. Now she'd been trapped in her fantasy. She looked down. Another black gondola left its mooring carrying lovers through the night. If she could go back in time...

Turning to face the crowd, she scanned the party for Sebastian. He'd left her side twenty minutes ago to take an urgent phone call from his aunt's doctor. Had that call been staged?

Not that Sadie needed a man to rescue her. She could take care of herself. But it would be nice to see him and his broad shoulders right about now.

Elaborate masks and costumes made it hard to tell who the bad guys were. Or how many. But it still appeared the satyr hunted alone.

She reviewed her options once more. She'd love to phone for help, but lifting her big skirt to remove the cell-phone strapped to the inside of her right thigh would cause too much commotion and give the satyr time to pounce. She fidgeted.

The satyr's stare burned the side of her head. So disgusting. No matter how this night ended, she'd hate the satyr mask forever.

The cacophony of voices speaking many languages and dialects grew louder. The party had hit its zenith.

At moments like this, adrenalin pushed her senses to the extreme. The crowd became one large pulsating body of humanity. She could feel and smell the longing of unfulfilled desires in the crowd. A transcendental moment before all hell broke loose.

Looking over her shoulder, she spied him ten yards away. His mouth was unusually empty of expression, as if he'd faced his existential wall and lost. His dark eyes glared. She grabbed the stone banister with both hands and scrambled to the top. Once on her knees she pulled herself to a standing position. The breeze cooled her skin as she found her balance like a gymnast.

People gasped. "Dio, Dio," one man cried. A murmur of concern spread through the crowd as they turned to look at her, the crazy woman

"Tell Sebastian Wilde I need him," she yelled at the wide-eyed group of people near her, hoping someone might know the popular art dealer and understand her message. At the very least, the people with their eyes on her would get the desperation of her dramatic act and call the police. The confusion created by her climb would make it harder for her stalker to pounce. She gritted her teeth, hoping the man in black would disappear into the shadows from which he'd oozed.

But he didn't. She exhaled, not realizing she'd been holding her breath. Pushing back his cloak, the stalker quickened his pace and moved to close the gap between them.

The top of the foot-wide marble railing had been built sturdily, and she could stand on it as long as she didn't look down. She most definitely couldn't look down. Edging to the east she focused on keeping her footing steady and breathing. She needed oxygen to fuel her muscles. She'd been trained to handle adrenalin rushes. Steady breathing—would do the trick. She could do this. As long as she didn't... Her right foot slipped. Damn the stupid shoes. She kicked one off, then the other. People below started yelling and looking up. The marble felt cool to her feet. Her skirt brushed the surface and she pulled it up with her hands.

"Look a woman is standing on the railing. Look," yelled a woman below. Other cries were muted as she focused on her step. Tunnel vision. Another sign of the adrenalin rushing through her system.

The people on the terrace pushed away from her, as if she might pull them over. No one wanted to be grabbed by a lunatic on a ledge. A white-haired dowager squared her shoulders and marched up to her reaching for her with a thin hand covered in blue veins. "Come down from there," she demanded like an old school marm. "Is it man trouble? Trust me dear, they aren't worth it."

Sadie shook her head. A slight gust of air brushed her shoulder as a shiny Ninja star sped past her skin, missing by an inch. Great, the satyr's a Mutant Ninja Turtle in disguise. She gripped the surface of the banister with her toes, an impossible task, but she tried all the same.

The older woman screamed. "Someone's attacking her," and ran back into the throng.

Could this night get any freaking worse?

As if in answer to her question, a second star whizzed by her mouth. This time it missed by half an inch. Sweet Jesus. Keep your balance Sadie. A familiar metallic taste flooded her mouth, her focus sharpened even more. Left foot, breathe, right foot... She talked her way forward, her muscles cramping from the strain.

It made no sense. What kind of man would throw Ninja weapons in the middle of a charity ball? He had to be either really desperate, really stupid, or... confident he could get away with it. As her former spy-boss Jeremiah once said: "Venice is a city where secrets hide for centuries." Sweat poured from her body drenching her bra and panties, which stuck to her like a second skin. She wiped at her eyes to see more clearly. Not looking down. She couldn't look down. She inched along. Surely someone would come and help her soon.

A third star. This time a freaking quarter inch away. The air whipped by her face, swishing as the disc sliced through it. The satyr-turtle neared.

And why Ninja discs? Hiro shuriken were not as deadly as made out in cartoons. The Samurai used them to distract their opponents so they could move in for the kill. Move in for the kill. Was that the man's agenda?

Screams and shouts filled the air. In the distance a siren blared. But it was all muted. She could see and feel only her body, the banister and her stalker.

Without thinking her eyes slid down, seeking an escape route. Damn it. She shouldn't look. She knew better. Nausea rose in her throat like a volcano. Damn she hated heights. Slick with sweat her hands reached out into the air to steady her body, which teetered as the rush of dizziness hit her head. Escape. She had to get off the banister.

But the wooziness in her head threatened her balance. Time to gain solid ground. Time to take the initiative. Reminding herself that when it comes to fighting nice girls finish dead, she took a deep breath and jumped back onto the balcony. She turned to face her assailant standing only three feet away. She hoped he didn't know she had training, because her talent would take him by surprise. In street fights anything goes. And it goes fast. She pushed her body past two people in her way, wanting the first move.

"Asshole," she screamed as she aimed her right foot straight for his balls.

Doubling over, he cried out.

Her second kick aimed for his head, but his hand caught her ankle and twisted her to the ground. Pain shot up her leg and into her hip. She lay on her back, watching as he raised his right fist to punch her.

But a large hand caught his arm.

Behind the satyr stood Sebastian Wilde. Her Sebastian, a giant of a man who looked like a modern Viking with long, sun-kissed blond hair that fell wild and loose to his shoulders. Tonight he dressed as a genie in purple silk. On his broad face he wore a silver mask that accentuated his pale blue eyes. Blue like the morning sky, they were the most intense eyes she'd ever seen. A shiver of recognition mingled with love mingled with relief ran through her body. Sebastian.

The satyr's body flew from hers as Seb pulled him away. She sat up to see her assailant grabbed by two security guards. Where had they been all this time? The whole incident had taken only a few minutes, but it had felt like eternity.

Sebastian reached down for her. "How do you get yourself into these situations?" he said. The ragged tone of his voice hit her like a ton of Ninja stars. That was the thing about Sebastian. She had to read between the lines to understand him. Torn between helping her up and kicking the shit out of her attacker, his voice took on a frustrated edge. A man of action, he didn't like being torn.

She let him help her up. These are the sorts of things she'd only figured out by dating him for six months. Dating? Do they even use that term these days? And if they did, did it come anywhere near explaining what they meant to each other? Why think about this now? Her body trembled.

Once on her feet, she tugged at her dress and brushed hair away from her sweaty face. "I didn't need rescuing," she said, not really meaning to say it out loud. The words just slid out.

He pulled her into his arms and his familiar scent hit her harder than a double-malt scotch on the rocks. "I did it for me," he whispered into her ear.

Her body continued shaking from exertion and adrenalin and the potent chemistry of Sebastian. It would be easy to stay in his embrace forever.

She couldn't. Not now. Pushing away from Seb, she took another look at her attacker. He'd been hand-cuffed, and the security team were marching him into the main building. Scanning his body from top to bottom she noticed something on his arm. "Wait," she called out to them. They turned and let her catch up. "Let me see," she said, pointing to the man's right wrist. The satyr fought, but the men forced his wrist towards her. A finely detailed tattoo, the size of an American quarter, marked his arm, The Eye of Horace inked in black, in the center of a green triangle. She'd never seen such a tattoo.

In one strong stroke she whipped off his mask, but she didn't recognize him. He had a round face with faint freckles and a receding chin. He looked unremarkable and not at all like an assassin, more like an overgrown boy scout. She locked his face into her memory. "Why?" she asked.

"We're watching you," he said in a staccato voice and then he collapsed. His face paled and turned pink. Cyanide! He must have had a suicide pill. The men tried to hold him up, but his body sagged between them. They helped him onto the floor of the terrace and took his pulse. It took four minutes for him to die.

CHAPTER 2

Amsterdam
September

*B*akari al Sharif stared at the
entrance of a rundown, hole-in-the-wall restaurant
called Arabian Nights, on a seedy, narrow, back
street in Amsterdam. Ignoring the rain falling solidly
on his head, he studied the place. His gut twisted.
Why here of all places?

He had no moral qualms about drugs or the
business of selling them, but this place with its
stained windows, peeling paint and faded sign
disgusted him. It looked sad, like a den of iniquity
that even the devil had neglected—a lair for lost
souls in the heart of a city known for debauchery. A
slimy underside of life. Why couldn't he find Khalid
Badru somewhere nice? The weight in his chest
grew heavier.

His people had searched for the young man
for six months. Now he stood only yards away from

him. This would be their first meeting. His heart raced.

As the broken front door opened, a middle-aged American couple sauntered out arm in arm, smiling and laughing. He envied their peace. Rainwater trickled inside the neckline of his black leather jacket and the cold soaked into the marrow in his bones. He shook his head, not quite ready to enter the building.

Would he ever feel ready? His body, numbed with exhaustion, muddled his thinking. He hadn't slept a full night since Djeserit had told him about Khalid. On her death bed she'd said things that echoed in his mind and in his heart like a curse. He had to go in, had to meet him, had to stop him.

With a quick hand motion he commanded his body-guard to stay outside. This meeting would be hard enough to face alone. He didn't want an audience.

Bakari strode across the threshold. The small room, filled with wooden tables, chairs and droopy-eyed people interested him little. The walls were stained brown, a remnant from the days when cigarette smoking had been allowed in public places. The air smelled thick and rancid, a mixture of soured food, sweat and weed. The rock'n'roll playing through small speakers on the wall, sounded scratchy as if it came from old vinyl records fished out of a dumpster. A man in the corner strummed a guitar, as if people listened to him. A middle aged woman dressed in a long skirt danced in the middle of the room. Her hips moved to a rhythm that didn't match the music, but called to anyone who would listen. The blond bartender with pink streaks in his hair cocked an eye at Bakari and nodded towards the back.

Bakari had an appointment.

He walked through the people examining them, like ants in an anthill. Khalid would be waiting. His assistant had set up a three o'clock meeting, had said it was for an out-of-town man wanting to know his future. He quickened his pace as he neared the closed, black door then stopped in front of it.

A sign the door read in English, "Know your future." Rusty hinges squeaked as he opened the portal. He swallowed. The man who'd haunted his mind for the last six months sat behind a circular wooden table like a regular guy.

At last! He'd found him. The young man beckoned for him to come in. Bakari closed the door and took his first good look at him.

The only light in the room came from a candle on the table, which cast shadows on the angular face of Khalid Badru, who sat motionless. The air seemed cleaner inside the room and the music muted, giving it the feeling of a cocoon. A cocoon in a lair of darkness. An interesting place to hide.

Stacked beside the candle were Djeserit's tarot cards. He'd watched her use them many times: a standard spirit deck she'd trimmed and personalized with an edge of gold paint. Bakari's gut wrenched.

"Sit down," said the young man in a commanding voice strong enough to control an army. He nodded towards the empty seat opposite.

Bakari walked closer and sat. Sweat sprang up along his backbone. He'd had half a year to think about what to say, and now he had no words. He just wanted to look at the young man.

Intelligent, dark eyes probed back at him and an uncomfortable silence swallowed the room. He was seventeen, but he looked twenty-five. The small muscles around his eyes held a rigid tightness, as if he'd seen enough in his short time on this earth to make him wary. His long black hair had been pulled back into a pony tail revealing a cleanly shaved face with a firm, masculine jawline, a feature which ran in his family. Bakari's throat constricted as he took in Khalid's cocoa-colored skin, which reminded him so much of Djeserit.

Bakari assessed people with speed and precision. In his business an accurate understanding of people was a matter of life and death. Khalid had a Frankenstein look about him, like a man not fully grown into himself, a man who could be dangerous, a shell waiting for its heart. Daring, possibly unstable, but surely not as dangerous as Djeserit had claimed.

Suspicion played across the light in the young man's eyes and he leaned his lanky body back in his chair. "My name is Khalid Badru. Do I know you?"

The words hit Bakari like a thousand grenades, unleashing a toxic mixture of regret and anger within. "Not yet."

Maybe he should have just had him killed, as his brother had suggested. No. That wouldn't be right. If anyone killed this man, it would have to be him. But the man was barely more than a boy. A boy with his blood. Bakari wanted to give him a chance.

As if reading the older man's thoughts, the younger man's eyes widened. "What do you want from me?"

The exact question he'd be asking, if he sat on that side of the table. But where to start? "A reading," Bakari said. "I'd like to know my future."

Khalid nodded slowly and for a minute he looked about to say something. Instead, he firmed his lips and lit a stick of cheap, incense. The smell drifted into the air in streams of smoke. He gave Bakari a dispassionate glance. "Shuffle the cards, old man."

Bakari reached for the deck. Why would the boy insult him? What did he know?

"Shuffle. Only if you dare," Khalid said.

A chill ran up Bakari's spine. He looked up from the cards and their eyes caught. The room tilted, twisted and distorted like a flowing, psychedelic hallucination and the pungent smell of the incense choked him. Bakari coughed and looked away. It was better not to look a seer in the eye.

"I mean you no harm," Bakari said, but that wasn't the complete truth. Maybe confronting a seer with the powers of Khalid in this way hadn't been a good idea. The man seemed more powerful than Djeserit.

"You are angry with me and I don't even know you." The words resonated through Bakari. How far into his mind could the man see?

"I am anxious about my future. That is all." He pulled out his wallet.

Khalid looked him over then glanced towards the west wall. "One thousand euro." His voice was flat and demanding.

Bakari lifted an eyebrow and stared at the young man.

"I am good at what I do."

Bakari pulled out the cash and placed it on the table. It disappeared instantly into the pocket of the seer. Then he fixed his eyes on Bakari and asked, "Are you sure you want to know your future? I cannot lie to you. I have taken an oath."

In answer to his question, Bakari gathered the tarot cards into his hands. He sensed their strange, ethereal warmth… and something else. The new owner of the cards had added his own power to them. They felt heavier and thicker. He shuffled the cards until his breathing returned to normal, then cut them into three piles and asked his silent question. He re-stacked the cards.

Like a cobra, in one fluid motion Khalid rose and raised his hands to the sky. The flickering light of the candle cast long shadows on his body. His face hardened. "I, coming forth as Amen, the hidden one."

The hair on the nape of Bakari's neck rose. In that moment Khalid looked so much like his mother. Had his power consumed him already?

From his pocket the seer pulled a black wand and waved it once in the air. "I am the keeper of Akashic Records. All of which is, and which shall be. Eternity and Everlastingness, open your portals." He put his large right hand on top of the cards. "May I fly like a golden hawk. May I see the truth revealed." He stood absolutely still. So still he no longer looked alive.

Bakari tried to take a deep breath, but the air came into his lungs in short gasps.

Khalid waved the wand once between them. "Searcher of Truth..."

Silence filled the room like a tomb. This was the moment when Djeserit would channel information from spirits on the other side, warn him of upcoming problems, tell him how his life would unfold. But this young man said nothing. Transfixed, Bakari waited.

The pupils of Khalid's eyes glazed over. He looked possessed. "It is you—"

Bakari clenched his fists. "Tell me what you see."

Khalid's face contorted, as if in pain. "You are my father." His hand holding the ebony wantd between them shook.,

"You and I are cursed."

CHAPTER 3

Venice

In her bare feet, Sadie stood on the cold surface of the palace terrace watching the paramedics carry the dead assassin away. His face, locked in a death mask, had twisted in his painful last moments, as if he saw hell awaiting him and wanted to turn back. But it was too late for him. Horror, shock and pain were embedded into his features. What a sad way to die.

Who the hell was he?

She glanced at Sebastian, who was overseeing the removal of the body. He caught her eyes but held them only for a moment. The hardness in his chin, the flatness in his pupils, the stiff movements of his body, all spoke of his seething anger, barely contained. They'd have another of their, 'you need to live a safer life' arguments later. This was not how she'd imagined her night with him.

The evening had started so well, had held so much promise. When the six foot five Sebastian, built like a warrior, picked her up at her hotel earlier, it seemed nothing could go wrong. That moment crystalized in her mind. She had wanted to jump him on the spot, but they didn't have time. They were expected to be at the opening of the charity event. People counted on them. Friends that mattered counted on them. Sex had to wait.

That seemed to be the main problem in their globe-trotting relationship. When they were together everything rocked, but their lives kept pulling them apart. Her modeling assignments took her all over the world, and while Sebastian spent most of his time in Amsterdam his art business took him all over Europe.

If she could freeze time and go back to the beginning of the evening she would. The night had gone to hell after that. She ran a hand across her brow, wiping the sweat away. Her breathing had slowed to normal and her shaking had stopped. The adrenalin in her system had run its course. Damn. Her eye makeup must be a mess.

The crowds who had kept their distance during the satyr's take-down moved in. "Signora, va tutto bene?" "Are you all right?" "Bent u goed?" Concern for her well-being blanketed her in many languages. Her tunnel vision faded and she took in the whole scene again. Someone in the crowd must have alerted security. Luckily, no one had been hurt.

She wiped at the sweat on her face again. Under a mask and layers of dress she felt exposed. She'd love to disappear. Right there, right then, on the spot. She needed to get away and assess the situation.

"Si. Si, grazie," she said. "Yes, oui, ja." Nodding, she gave them her cover-girl smile, knowing it looked haggard; but it was all she had for them and she wanted to give them something. They had saved her, after all, and being a part of humanity after someone has tried to kill you felt good. Real good.

She looked towards the last speaker, Sebastian's Belgian friend Gregor who had organized the party. She had never warmed to his continental style. A GQ handsome man in the diamond business he found philanthropy good for his bottom line. Normally he looked Wall Street confident and Spanish bullfighter aggressive, but not right now. A deep line creased his brow and the corners of his straight, thin mouth quivered. "I'm so sorry," he said. "I don't know why there weren't security men out here. His face paled. Sebastian told me..."

Three hotel waiters encouraged the crowds to move away.

"Told you what?"

Sebastian walked over to them. Clearly he had heard her words. He sent his friend a dagger stare, but it was too late. His secret was out.

"To keep you safe at all costs."

Sadie turned and squared her shoulders in front of Sebastian. He wouldn't have told his friend details about her past, but he did tell him to take extra precautions, something she'd asked he never do.

Sadie didn't want her cover blown and besides—she could take care of herself. But Sebastian, the stubborn Frisian, was hell bent on protecting her. Why couldn't he listen to her? Her hands went to her hips, heat rushed to her face and she glared at him. "I'm going back to my hotel. Don't follow me."

"Sadie? Mijn liefje."

She didn't wait to hear what he had to say. Her muscles involuntarily trembled, from the aftermath of the adrenalin, her head ached and anger squeezed her gut. Tonight, on their six-month anniversary, she'd wanted romance. Instead, she'd been hunted by a satyr and betrayed by her lover. In bare feet she waded through the throng to the staircase and made her way down to the canal. Faces turned and voices came towards her with kindness, but she kept moving. She growled as she lifted her gown and hopped into a boat taxi to make her escape.

"We're watching you." She recalled her stalker's words. Her stomach sank. Why?

His distinctive tattoo bothered her. The Eye of Horace in a green triangle. What the hell did that mean? It looked like a membership insignia of some kind. Did he belong to a gang with a thing for Egyptian symbols? A weird religious sect?

The ass-hole could be connected to the power hungry Egyptian, arms-dealer Bakari al-Sharif, the man she'd let slip through her fingers. Not a pleasant thought. Dangerous, violent, volatile and horny. Yes, horny. She hadn't noticed any such signature on Bakari's people. It probably had nothing to do with him.

Sadie sat in the stern of the boat. As the soft evening breeze cooled her face she considered doing an Internet search for information. But Google had its limitations, not to mention its trolls. To get the best answers in the fastest possible way, she had to contact Langley. Langley, Virginia, as in the headquarters of the Central Intelligence Agency.

Sebastian would be furious. Her inner goddess who'd been working on inner-peace would be pissed too. She hadn't talked with anyone from "the Company" for six months, not since she walked out of her handler's office and told him not to call her. And he didn't.

It had all made sense then. But now?

The taxi slid down a side canal to a back street near the quaint inn she liked to stay in when she spent time in Venice, the Bella Giornata. The sight of the beautiful old place always warmed her heart, made her feel at home.

Barefoot, wearing a rumpled Marie Antoinette gown and smeared makeup, she climbed out of the boat with the dignity and class of royalty. Projecting the dream had been part of her training, both as an international model and as a spy. When you project what people want to see, you have them.

Three couples strolled down the narrow road chatting with one another. She slipped past them and slid into the back alley that led to her inn. Twenty yards down the alleyway, she arrived at the Bella Giornata, with its tall, shuttered windows and wrought-iron balconies holding boxes overflowing with flowers. The pink and purple blooms cascaded down the side of the hotel towards the narrow alley twenty yards below. The inn was not the ritziest place in town, but it was her private get-away. During her first trip to Venice ten years ago, she'd stumbled upon it. Since then she had returned at least once a year. It was an exotic sanctuary that collected memories. Delicious memories.

The first moment she saw Venice, she'd fallen in love with the city, the people, the tasty cicheti, the Veneto wine and most of all the exotic charm of a quaint cosmopolitan city that had once been an empire powerful enough to rule the civilized world. There was no place on earth like Venice.

History seeped through the walls of the palaces lining the Grand Canal around which the city had been built. Secrets, memories, love and passion. Italians were all about passion and Venetians kicked it up to another level.

The night was still warm, and the air inside her room was hot and sticky. She took off her layers of sweaty clothing and hit the shower. The sooner she could get her body fully back to normal the safer she'd be. She groaned. Thinking like a spook again.

Hot water pummeled her sore muscles. Her breathing deepened. Her mind cleared. Her anger faded. She increased the water temperature until steam filled the room. She needed this. After five more minutes she got out and wrapped herself in a thick white robe.

The night had had such a promising beginning. That was what angered her the most: paradise imagined, then lost. Her mind returned to when Sebastian had arrived at her door, her super-sized man with a killer smile oozing virility. At that moment, Sadie thought her night would be filled with love and passion, a perfect beginning to their anniversary celebration.

Always full of surprises, Sebastian dressed in a genie costume, dropped to one knee and looked up at her. His eyes as blue as the morning sky in April danced with mischief. Her first thought had been: Is he going to propose? Nah! But her heart leaped into her throat. She'd thought about getting hitched to him, more often than she would admit to anyone, but even though she loved Sebastian more than she thought humanly possible, jumping into the institution-thing, with papers and pomp, didn't feel right. Been there, done that. Her bottom lip had slipped between her teeth as she waited for him to speak.

He took her hand in his. With his deep baritone voice that kicked her libido into overdrive, he said, "I am your genie for the night. You have three wishes. I am yours to command." She laughed. This was so like Sebastian. He had a wicked sense of humor in and out of bed. Good timing too. Impeccable timing. The kind that made counting the number of orgasms she had in one night impossible.

Three wishes from him made her blush from her little toes to the top of her head and back to her clit. A proposition no sane woman would refuse. She pulled him into her suite. They kissed long and hard. If they hadn't had so many layers of costume on they would have done more. But they were expected at the gala, charity ball.

After that... her night shredded to rat-shit.

Three wishes. She'd been thinking about the first one when she first spotted her would-be assassin. Her mind shifted gears to that moment, and her emotions hit hard. Time to get serious.

After pacing the length of the room five and a half times, she retrieved her cell-phone. And hesitated. Did she really want to re-enter that other world? She'd enjoyed being a model and having a guy who loved her. Did she really want to risk all that? Her fingers moved without further thought. She only had one good move.

Jeremiah answered after one ring. "Hi sugar." His southern accent, steady and deep, bounced off her backbone. The infamous spy-master, Jeremiah Cole, her former CIA handler, the man who'd taught her how to be a hot-shot spook. He didn't sound the least surprised to hear her voice.

Sinking into one of the two deep leather chairs in her suite, she imagined him on the other end of the call. A fit, mature man, aging well, with salt-and-pepper hair and clothes that made him look more like a librarian than a seasoned expert in all shades of espionage. She'd used his personal cell-phone number, but he was probably at work. He pretty well lived there, feeding on the intrigues and secrets of the world. A shudder ran through her. She pulled her robe tighter.

Surrounded by computer monitors and his chess set, the man was a legend. His intense gray eyes would study the screens as he spoke taking in information from around the world, but he would hear every word she said, every nuance and implication she made; and worst of all—he would hear all the stuff she didn't say.

In his fifties, he used a paternal tone of voice which annoyed her. At least she squared it in her mind as paternal. But it could have been something more. Not a good time to be contemplating that.

"Cole," she said.

Silence is hard to interpret on a phone. It hung between them like a solid black curtain for a moment. "How are the cheekbones?" he asked.

Smiling she leaned her head back. The first day they met she'd told him the only reason she'd become a famous model was that she had good bones. They were in his office. He'd been drinking tea and it spurted out of his mouth. It was the only time she could remember him acting so... human. "Sadie," he'd said, "as a man I have to tell you, people are looking at more than your cheekbones." Since then he'd teased her about them. She sighed. Teasing wasn't a bad place to start.

"I'm in Venice. One hour ago, I was at a charity ball on the top of the Danieli and a man dressed in a satyr costume stalked me." She gave him all the details in as few words as possible. That's how he'd trained her to communicate, but in the past she would add unnecessary details to annoy him. But not tonight.

"Sounds like Venice."

Sadie could feel his smile. "The guy was agile and skilled at throwing Ninja stars."

"Are you hurt?

"No."

"The man?"

"Dead. Cyanide. He died in less than four minutes and I wasn't able to get information, but..."

The silence resumed. How much did she really want to tell him? Being connected to that world of shadows had a price. She had thought—hoped—she had left it behind.

He broke the quiet. "Why are you calling me?"

Just like Cole. Right to the point. "Two reasons. As the security men held him, I noticed a quarter-sized tattoo on his wrist and moved closer to get a better look. It had the Eye of Horace in black, inked into the middle of a green triangle."

She waited for Cole to respond, but he didn't. Probably too busy putting the image into a computer search. So she continued. "Before they hauled him away the would-be assassin said to me, 'We're watching you.'"

"Eye of Horace, green triangle, stalked, got it. Anything else?"

"What do you think?"

"I don't like men throwing weapons at you, sugar. And yes, the incident is probably related to your life with us. You should be concerned. I'll contact the Venetian police and do some research into the symbols, but..."

"But?"

"Just a hunch."

That was another thing about master spy Jeremiah. He had wickedly good hunches.

"Shoot."

"You got somebody mad, real mad. You're in danger.I'll be in touch."

"You got somebody mad, real mad. You're in danger. I'll be in touch."

CHAPTER 4

Sebastian threw his key card on the hotel dresser. It made a light thunk and bounced. He wanted to punch something. How could the night go so fucking wrong, after all his planning? He even put on a stupid purple costume just to please her. He'd brought her flowers, offered her three wishes... It was supposed to be a perfect night.

Ripping off his cape he paced the room. *Everything will be okay. Everything has to be okay.* He couldn't lose her. His chest tightened. His intentions had been good. She had to see that. He'd wanted her to remember their six month anniversary forever. That's why he'd agreed to meet her in Venice. Women like *forever* don't they? But Sadie was so bloody... Sadie. A lover's gift, burned in his pocket. *Godverdomme.*

And who the hell was the satyr? How did he elude security? Why did he kill himself? It all smelled of trouble. He didn't want trouble to touch her ever again.

If anyone could identify the stalker it would be his best friend, Xander van der Valk who ran an international art crime investigation business from Amsterdam. He had connections everywhere in the world. Seb grabbed his cell-phone and punched in his friend's number.

"What did she say?" Xander asked.

"I didn't get to ask her."

Silence.

"I'm sending you three pictures. The first is an asshole's fingerprints. I got them from the local police. The guy tried to grab Sadie at the party. He threw fucking Ninja stars at her as she tried to escape. When we took him down, he swallowed a cyanide pill. The second picture is of the guy, dead, and the third is a close-up of the tattoo on his arm."

"Is Sadie all right?" Concern anchored his friend's deep voice.

"Yeah," Seb hesitated, "but she's pissed at me, because Gregor told her I'd insisted on extra security for her."

Xander laughed long and loud.

Sebastian grumbled.

"Buddy, you don't get it," said Xander.

"What's there to get? I tried to keep her safe and she gets all bitchy."

"Extra security for Sadie is a good idea. Letting her know about it is another thing."

"I've never seen her so angry. She…" He stopped. His chest so tight it made it hard to say more.

"I get it," said Xander. "She doesn't want her cover blown and she thinks she can take care of herself."

"I just want to protect her."

"Yeah, big guy, I understand. But your woman is fiercely independent and used to looking after herself. You know her story. She's a force to be reckoned with."

Sebastian groaned. "She'd climbed onto the palace railings to escape from him. And then she attacked him. He had her on the ground and was about to punch her when I caught his arm. I don't care what she says, she needs me."

Silence.

"Xander?"

"I don't recognize the man in the picture, but I'll run his prints through my data base. If nothing comes up, I'll contact Seamus at Interpol."

"Thanks," said Sebastian.

"Did you give her three wishes?"

"Yeah, she liked that part."

"I'm betting she's thinking about them right about now. Give her an hour to let the effects of the adrenalin flush out of her system, and yours, then call her."

"I..."

"Don't fuck it up Sebastian. You two are meant for each other."

The line went dead.

CHAPTER 5

Amsterdam

*T*rying to appear calm, Bakari
looked at his son standing before him in his
ceremonial robe. His black wand trembled in the air
between them. *If only I could think of an easy way to
do this.* His mind reeled with thoughts and his chest
tightened with emotion until he thought it would
burst out his ears. There were things that needed to
be said. He prided himself on being a good
negotiator, but his well-honed skills were useless in
this situation.

Khalid hesitated, breaking the rhythm of his
performance. He lowered his wand. "Why have you
come?" His deep voice echoed in the small room.

Bakari took a breath. The smell of the cheap
incense burned the insides of his nostrils. "I didn't
know about you. If I had known..." He sighed. "If I
had known I had a son I would have been part of
your life."

Khalid lifted his wand and waved it lazily in the air as if he were conducting a symphony. "You want to play daddy?" The sarcasm in his voice cut the air between them. The glaze over his eyes drifted away in the flickering candle light, like mist evaporating in the morning light. He looked like a young man once again, an angry young man.

"I don't ignore my responsibilities." Bakari said. "You are my son. I want to do what is right." He firmed his jaw and straightened his back.

Khalid sat in the chair opposite, holding his stare. "How did you find out about me?"

"Djeserit told me."

"She's dead."

"Yes," Bakari said. "She called me to her death bed to tell me about you. I held her hand as she died"

Silence stole the room.

Khalid touched the Tarot cards before him. "I see the two of you in a narrow alleyway. Amsterdam. It smells like Amsterdam. You had been drinking. A rat skitters by. She..."

Bakari remained quiet while his son replayed his past, his inception, unfolding in his mind.

Khalid opened his eyes. "She took you."

"Yes. Your mother wanted you to have my blood." Bakari didn't want to discuss the erotic details of that night with his son. There had been an animal passion between him and Khalid's mother, hotter than he had ever experienced. There had also been magic. In her last moments, Djeserit, admitted she'd put him under a sorcerer's spell and ravaged him.

Khalid opened his eyes. "Tell me why?" His lean face thinned.

"Why?"

"Why you?"

Bakari smiled. The boy obviously hadn't been impressed with his physical appearance. Bakari opened his hands. "I grew up in Cairo. My family— our family—was dirt poor. I made millions dealing arms around the world to change that. I don't want any one in my family to go hungry again. I've let nothing stop me. I'm not proud of everything I've done, but I did what I had to do for my family." He swallowed. "My younger brother now runs the business. Blood is what counts. We are wealthy and we will take care of you."

"And you only slept with my mother once?"

Bakari firmed his lips. "I didn't even know it was her."

"It felt like an erotic nightmare to you." Khalid laughed. "My mother possessed ancient powers and she knew how to use them."

"Yes."Bakari leaned forward. "Over the years, her sight helped me achieve my goals. The truth is I could never have been as successful as I am without her."

"And now you want to use me?"

Bakari's gut twisted. Use? Such a harsh word. He would never get used to talking to seers. Other people could be fooled into believing whatever he wanted them to believe, but not Khalid or his mother. They had an unerving gift of sight. After a long minute Bakari said, "I want three things."

"Three?" The corners of Khalid's mouth turned up slightly as if he wanted to smile, but wouldn't let himself. He leaned back in his chair and for a moment looked like a bored and rebellious teenager.

"First, and foremost I want to be your father and help you in any way I can. Money, family... a home."

Khalid scrunched up his mouth as if Bakari's words rotted his brain.

Bakari waited.

"You've never been part of my life and I'm not sure I want you messing in it now."

"I hope to change your mind. You could leave this dump and return to Cairo with me—a rich man."

"And? What is your second request? What will my new found wealth cost me?"

Bakari held up his hand. "I need your sight. Your sister's life depends upon it."

Khalid grimaced. "A sister?" The fine muscles in his cheeks twitched.

"Rashida, your blood sister, is dying of cancer. Blood fights for blood. I've used a special amulet with ancient power your mother helped me find to keep her alive. But now her health is fading once again. I need your help to save her."

Light flickered across Khalid's dark eyes for a second. Had Bakari reached his heart?

Khalid said, "And third?"

Bakari exhaled noisily. "I'll leave that for later. Tell me how to save Rashida."

Khalid closed his eyes and a cold stillness filled the room. Color drained from his skin and ripples of dark energy crossed his expression as the tiny muscles of his face tightened, then loosened, then tightened again. Bakari looked at his watch and waited.

Five minutes later the color of his son's cheeks deepened and he opened his eyes. "There may be a way."

Bakari's chest tightened and he leaned forward. "I will do anything to get it."

"It won't be easy."

"My life is never easy."

CHAPTER 6

Venice

*S*adie spent the night tossing, turning and swearing. Her love for Sebastian pulled her one way, her need to be her own person pulled the other. Not a new conflict, but one that had come to a head at the charity ball. Some anniversary present! They'd planned to spend two romantic weeks together in Venice. And now... She wanted to punch him.

Soft, pink pre-dawn light bled through her bedroom window. Someone knocked on her door. Could she pull the covers over her head and pretend she wasn't there? She was too old for that crap. Dressed in a white cotton nightgown, she slid over to the door, looked through the spy hole to make sure it was him, then let him in.

Sebastian, wearing ripped, faded-blue jeans, an open-collar white shirt and a blue cotton sports coat strode in. His long hair had been pulled back into a pony tail. He hadn't shaved and the roughness of his stubble made her long to feel it against her body. Lines creased the edges of his blue eyes drooping with fatigue. She wasn't the only one who hadn't slept last night and that pleased her. The air between them electrified with unspoken emotion. They looked at each other for a full minute.

Sebastian broke the silence. *"Mijn liefje*, I have so much I want to say and I don't know where to begin or how to say it, so you'll understand me. I love you Sadie, more than I have ever loved any woman before. I want you to be a part of my life…"

She nodded. None of this was new.

"But…"

Sadie's eyes welled with tears. But? Were they really doing this? Were they about to break up? She reached for his hand, hoping the connection would steady them.

Light reflected from his soft blue eyes. "But," he continued, "I want to protect you. It's only natural." The way his six-foot-five body towered above hers emphasized his words. He wanted to be her man, her protector.

Sadie growled. She wanted him to be her lover. And sweet Jesus he was good at that. But she didn't want this. "Why can't you understand me? I'm trained to take care of myself, and I've done just fine on my own for thirty years."

His jaw tightened. "But do you want to be on your own?"

That did it. A tear spilled from her right eye. "No honey, I want to be with you. But you have to respect who I am."

"You said you were done with fighting and all the fucking crap that surrounds the CIA, but the way you're acting I'm not so sure. Last night..."

"Last night?"

"I saw the old Sadie back."

Her breath caught. He was right. She had stopped being a spook six months ago. Last night that world came back to her in an instant. A part of her that she had shut down came alive, fully alive, when she fought for her life. The thrill of living on the edge had surged through her veins. "I did what I had to do, nothing more."

"Just like a well-trained spy."

She couldn't deny that and wasn't about to apologize for it. "Do they know who the guy was?"

Sebastian shook his head.

"I contacted Jeremiah, but he hasn't gotten back to me yet."

"Jeremiah? *Godverdomme*. You said you were through with that life." His cheeks reddened.

"But that life may not be through with me."

"Sadie." His breathing was loud and labored, as though controlling his feelings took every ounce of his energy.

"Stop, and listen to me. Yes, I was furious with Jeremiah for not telling me everything about the Anubis op, but what employee doesn't get mad at their boss? It was a misunderstanding and the whole need-to-know culture of the CIA sucks. Really sucks. But putting that aside..."

"Aside?"

She held up her hand to stop him from saying more. "I believe in the CIA and the work it does to keep America safe. And I..." She took a deep breath.

"Miss the life." She hadn't fully realized it until she said it. But there it was.

"Fuck."

"Besides, Jeremiah is my best source for information. I had to contact him. It's a matter of personal safety and for all I know national security."

"I have Xander and Seamus at Interpol working on it." Sebastian's voice turned cool. "You must have known I would contact them."

She shook her head. Jeremiah had access to more databases than they did and perhaps even more important he had the unparalleled sharp mind of a master spy. There was no better analyst of information than Cole. She liked Sebastian's friends, but they were no match for him.

Sebastian grimaced. "I'm sorry if I wounded your pride by hiring extra security, but I believed it was necessary. I want you to be safe. That's something you'll have to learn to live with if you want to be with me. I can't have anything happen to you."

Sadie rolled her eyes. "Those extra precautions could blow my cover and make me more vulnerable. Look, if you want to be with *me*, it's got to be on my terms."

"Your terms?" His voice rose. "Your terms?" His face became so red she thought it would explode.

Instead he turned and walked out of the room leaving the door wide open.

CHAPTER 7

Amsterdam

In the small room he called his chambers, Khalid rose to his feet. He waved his black wand in the air and listened for the sacred stillness to fill the room. His father sitting at the table in front of him, had asked him to find a way to save his daughter, Khalid's sister. Exhaling, Khalid focused on the task.

Or at least, he tried to. His mind slid off-center, trying to comprehend what had taken place in the last half hour. When he was a boy he'd dreamed of meeting his father. But now? The moment wasn't anything like his dreams.

He'd never imagined his father would turn out to be Bakari al-Sharif, the famous, international arms dealer. His mother had kept that knowledge from him.

An Egyptian, power-hungry criminal. What the hell was he going to do with him? Khalid looked at the square built man who had the same chin and eyes as his own. He searched his face and body for more similarities, but nothing more seemed to connect them.

The man was a stranger and should stay that way. Bakari's violent nature oozed from his pores. Khalid could smell the vicious crimes he had committed to remain on top of his world.

He didn't need this man. Not now, not ever.

The arcane blood of his mother's family ran strong in him, the blood of the Egyptian adept, of sorcerers and psychics and healers. With practice he could perfect his skills. With practice he'd learn pure magic and become the most powerful man alive.

His father had no place in that future. He was a mere mortal stuck in the tawdry rut of ordinary living. He said his mother chose to mate with him for his strength, but Khalid couldn't see any strength to admire in the man's eyes, or his mind. He may be worth millions, but he smelled of weaknesses and, after his death, he would be soon forgotten. While Khalid would be remembered forever.

But for now, he would give his father what he wanted, his future in his hand.

Khalid lifted his eyes to the heavens then turned them inwards. "Brothers of Darkness heed my call. Open my mind that I may hear you. Let me fly like a falcon through the darkness and merge into the light of the dawn. Let me know what I must know." His hand, holding the black wand, trembled more than ever before. Perhaps he'd misjudged his father. The energy in the room thickened, and darkness pressed in on him until he gasped for breath. "Open thy portals and take your servants in." Everything went black.

A moment later he opened his eyes. His father still sat on the other side of the table, staring back at him with wide eyes. Sweat flowed down his olive-skinned face. But everything around them blurred. It was as if they existed in one moment and one space in time and their surroundings had faded into shadows. He swallowed, tasting bile in his spit.

"Son, perhaps you shouldn't do this." Bakari said. Was that concern in his voice? *Too little, too late old man.*

"I am in control," said Khalid. But listening to his voice, he knew that the one in control came from beyond.

"Your face has turned white; your eyes are glazed and darkened; you look... unwell. I'm worried for you," Bakari said.

Khalid laughed and listened to his thunderous voice echo in the small fetid space between them.

"Your mother didn't look like this when she told me my future. Nor did she call to the darkness. I fear you're going beyond your capabilities..."

"Yes."

"Places a man should not go."

"For you, Father, I will venture into the unknown. Together we can handle whatever lies in wait for us."

"No, Khalid. Listen to me. Your pride will push you too far. I know this. My pride let me do things I should never have done. You need to think about what you're doing. It's not too late for you. This is what your mother warned me about. She didn't want you..."

"Didn't want me to do what?"

Bakari's dark-skinned face turned white. "To become a black wizard."

Khalid laughed again. "But don't you see? I became one the day I killed her. The gods do not take kindly to matricide."

Bakari put his head in his hands. "My God, what have we done?"

"You and my mother created a powerful man who fears no mortal."

"Khalid, listen to yourself. You are made of flesh and bones. You are not a god. Do not tempt the balance of the universe with your words."

"Daddy," he said, "do you really think you can stop me?"

"I'm begging you, on your mother's grave, to think about what you're doing."

A strong wave of energy bolted through Khalid's body from the ground up to the top of his head. He gasped and listened as another voice spoke through him.

"Destiny will not be denied. You both have debts to pay." The voice spoke so deeply it made his insides shudder. "And you will pay them."

Bakari sat up. "I will pay any debt as long as I can save my daughter Rashida."

"There is an amulet, a sacred scarab that belonged to Tutankhamen. It has the power you seek."

"Where?" Bakari's voice croaked.

"It will soon be revealed in England."

"Can I get it?"

"Yes, but it won't be easy. There will be forces trying to stop you. You need to bring it back to Egypt where it belongs. It will help Rashida."

"And my son?"

Silence filled the room.

"My son?"

"Is filled with so much darkness he doesn't know he needs to fight it."

"Can the amulet help him too?"

Khalid's mouth opened wide. A rumbling sound like the roar of a wave crashing on the shore, drowned the room with its intensity. Then it stopped, and stillness filled the space again.

"Khalid are you all right?" Bakari asked leaning towards him. The young man had turned whiter than a ghost and his body shook as if it couldn't quite settle.

Khalid blinked. "You have your answers, old man. Now, leave me alone."

CHAPTER 8

Langley, Virginia

As Sadie walked through the maze of cubicles to get to Jeremiah's office, she avoided making eye contact with anyone. She didn't want to chat... in case it softened her resolve. With her chin tilted up, she did her model's walk.

Confrontations had never been her thing. Her CIA shrink said her avoidance behavior was typical of a child with an alcoholic parent. Whatever. She'd rather skirt a fight than be in the middle of it, especially if it involved emotion.

If only there'd been another way to get the information. Jeremiah, her former handler, wouldn't tell her what she wanted to know over the phone. He'd insisted on seeing her. Coming back to the office sucked—big time.

Even in her happiest days working for the CIA she dreaded entering this building. It wasn't about dealing with the people who lived in the shadows, though they could be pretty weird; it was the clinical atmosphere of the business side of this life that irked her. Being a big organization it made sense that reports had to be written, read, sorted, stamped and filed. Some deleted. But the business of planning and cataloging acts of espionage, layered in lies and blood, was more like an elaborate dance of the seven veils than a telling of the truth. The elusiveness of it all bent reality. Nothing on the paper in this building resembled the truth.

The air smelled dusty, like the ventilation system hadn't been overhauled in a while. The smell of budget cuts. The CIA was a world in itself, housed in this building with decorated walls that attempted to normalize the operation as a business, but that was impossible. The deception that was its lifeblood corrupted the essence of the system. It was a place set on self-destruct, an institution sworn to protect the nation that could not protect itself. There were too many people with secrets; too many secrets. They had just made huge changes in its structure, but its intrinsic problem could never be addressed.

Why had it taken a run-in with an arms-dealer to make this clear to her?

Her stilettos clicked on the linoleum. There had always been spies, but fitting them into a bureaucratic engine as large as the CIA bothered her. Too many times the acquired knowledge backfired on the wrong people. They called it collateral damage. What a pile of crap. When her bosses had chosen to deceive her, to send her into an operation blindfolded, she had quit.

But now she was back.

Sadie considered the official motto of the CIA: The Work of a Nation. The Center of Intelligence. *Oxymoron time.* Clearly, they thought they could do more than they could. She'd been guilty of that, thinking that with her cover-girl face she could get any information they needed.

Sadie preferred the company's unofficial motto, the one she'd carried close to her heart during her work as a spook: "And you shall know the truth and it shall set you free." Finding the truth took digging, and that's what undercover agents did. That statement rang true in her head; or at least it had before the Anubis op. She balled her fists then released them; balled and released them again. When did this hallway grow so long?

Jeremiah waved her in through his open door. Sadie didn't hesitate.

"I'm glad you came in, sugar," he said in his southern drawl, as she clicked the door shut behind her.

She sat in the chair opposite him. Everything looked the same as the last time she'd been there. Same six photos, in black frames, on the wall. Her eyes focused on the one of Jeremiah standing beside President Bill Clinton on a small boat, holding a downrigger, fishing rod in his hand. The photo had been signed: "Thanks for the memories... Bill." The same chessboard with pieces in place sat to the right of his keyboard. It looked like a bold opening for the white team. Same computer screens buzzing, as information flowed through them like water in a river. Same Jeremiah Cole.

He was an intense middle-aged man who held you prisoner with his charismatic gray eyes from the moment you arrived. He wore a Wall Street suit, but beneath it his perfectly, pressed cotton shirt was open at the collar. She'd never seen him wear a tie. His thin lips smiled at her slightly, but no real emotion. *Did he have any feelings about how their relationship ended?* An enigma of a man. The jagged scar that ran down his neck from below his left ear to his collar chilled her to the bone. This was a master spy with years of experience in the field. "I have the information you want," he said.

"Why didn't you send it to me?"

"I need to talk to you."

Sadie resisted the impulse to squirm under his gaze. "About what?"

"I need you back."

Sadie's eyebrows rose so high she could feel her pupils stretch. She opened her mouth and was about to say, "Not in this century," when he held up his hand for her to stop.

"Listen to me."

She shook her head. "Give me a break. You want to feed me more lies peppered with patriotic crap?"

Jeremiah smiled. "Again, I'm sorry we didn't tell you everything about Bakari al-Sharif. But I have orders to follow, and my orders were to tell you only what you needed to know. The complex relationship between the agency and that arms dealer wasn't part of that."

"Since when did you follow all the rules?"

He leaned back with a small smile. "Fair enough. I could have told you despite my orders. But I thought it best you didn't know. In hind sight, it was a bad call on my part."

"Damn straight." He didn't look one bit remorseful. Lying to people he put in danger was just part of his job.

"Giving you one objective made you more effective. The other stuff really didn't matter. We wanted to take him down before he broke into the museum, and it had nothing to do with our former deals with him."

"And I didn't succeed."

"Maybe not that time, but..."

Her eyes widened. That time? "What the hell, Jeremiah?"

"Bakari al-Sharif, code-name Anubis, is planning another raid." His voice went low with suspense, as if he were an announcer on a wildlife documentary talking about a lion ready to pounce on its prey.

"His daughter?"

Jeremiah nodded. "Rashida's health is failing."

"So he's after more amulets to keep her alive?"

"I think he believes that. Yes. And, Sadie, not only are you one of our best operatives, you are the only one who's ever got close to him."

"And survived." She remembered too well how Bakari buried his third wife's head in the desert. A shiver ran up her spine.

"You can reach him." He hesitated. "Talk to him. Find out..."

"Yeah, yeah, groom him. Get him to tell me his secrets so I can pass them on to the Company." She shook her head. "You want me to be a honey pot, but it won't work. He already knows I'm a spook. I'm just lucky he let me live."

Jeremiah steepled his hands on his desk. "I suspect he has... feelings for you."

Silence. How did Jeremiah always figure things out? She hadn't said any of that stuff in her final report. Hadn't even suggested it. But Jeremiah was bull's-eye-right. Damn him. Bakari al-Sharif had the hots for her.

After a minute Sadie said, "Okay, this is the way I see it. Rashida got better by the grace of God and maybe because she believed in the power of the ancient good luck charm her father brought her. The amulet returned to Egypt where I believe it belongs. No one died. Well, except Delilah who made the fatal mistake of crossing al-Sharif. I consider it a successful mission. Things get messy in our business."

"Battle. A successful battle, more or less. But the war isn't over. Al-Sharif wants more power. We can't let him continue to steal priceless treasures."

"Bakari al-Sharif will always want more power. That's who he is. And what you call treasure, he calls power."

"Then you know we must stop him."

She shook her head again. "I'd like to stop all the bad people in the world, but I no longer think that's possible; and more importantly I no longer think I have to be the one to do it. I don't feel invincible anymore and I don't believe the CIA has the right to do half of what it's doing."

Jeremiah lowered his hands, leaned back and gripped the edge of his desk. "Then let me tell you about your stalker." As the tone of his voice darkened her stomach tightened.

"The man with the distinctive tattoo?"

"Yeah. The tattoo is the insignia of the KOTL, the Keepers of the Light. Pronounced like hotel except starting with a k."

"Never heard of them."

He grimaced. "Until I researched the tattoo, I thought they were just parts of ancient lore, shadowy creatures in someone's overactive imagination. Their sworn mission is to protect the arcane knowledge of the Emerald Tablets."

"Emerald tablets? Never heard of them, either." She shifted her butt in the seat.

"It's the stuff of ancient legends. People believe that etched on emerald stones are documents that contain the essence of Heretica, the ancient Egyptian and Greek wisdom texts. Translations exist today, reportedly handed down through history, but no one knows what happened to the original tablets."

"Let me guess: except for the KOTL."

"You got it. They believe their sole purpose on earth is to protect the ancient texts and the wisdom contained within them."

"Sounds like a case for Indiana Jones."

"Perhaps, but we don't have him. We have Mata Hari." His smile spread. "You're our secret, seductive weapon."

She shook her head. "Tell me about the tat."

"The Eye of Ra symbol comes from ancient Egypt and is a symbol for protection, royal power and good health. The green coloring of the triangle represents the Emerald Tablets. The three points on the triangle refer to the power structure within their organization. The top vertex points to the light, the left to Thoth, the god of knowledge and wisdom, and the right to themselves, the keepers."

"Okay. So?"

"So they aren't the sort of people you want watching you."

She wriggled her toes, trapped in heels. "Why would they want to?"

"They are a cult. Cults are dangerous. Whenever you get a bunch of zealots following a leader because they believe in something intangible you got trouble. This group believes their mission is to ensure the safety and preservation of the tablets, which they claim to have locked away. They don't make much noise, but we know they exist and we know they can be ruthless when crossed. Last month we found one of their leaders disemboweled. He'd set up a meeting with us to reveal information. I'm guessing it had to do with you. Somehow, Sugar, you have come onto their radar and they see you as a threat."

"I hadn't heard of the Emerald tablets before now. How could I possibly be a threat to them?" She threw up her hands. "It sounds like the stuff of campfire stories. It could all be crap. I bet no one has ever seen the stones."

"There are some who believe they were written by the god Thoth, who then became the ruler of Atlantis." Jeremiah's eyes twinkled as he kept his voice steady.

Sadie rolled her eyes. "And I'm the reincarnation of an Egyptian tomb cat?" She shrugged her shoulders. "What could I possibly have to do with wisdom texts?"

Jeremiah's focus shifted to his chess board and he moved his black knight. "To them, obviously something. Something worth killing you for. Don't dismiss that. There is power in believing something is true, even if it's not. They could, for example, kill you because they see you as a threat. Remember your stalker killed himself to hide what he knew."

"But why?" She felt her chest tighten.

"Bakari al-Sharif? Could he have a connection?"

She didn't respond.

"Just listen to me. Al-Sharif's been gathering amulets because he believes they give him power. But I suspect that upsets the KOTL, because they believe he's threatening the natural world order or maybe because of something written on their tablets."

"You're guessing."

"Yup, but you know I'm good at it. I look at the facts and ride them as far as they'll take me, then I make a calculated hypothesis. It makes sense. I figure they've been watching al-Sharif and found you. Now they're watching you."

"So throwing Ninja stars at me as I totter on top of a balcony railing was an elaborate warning from a group of fanatic wing-nuts worried I'm about to upset the balance of life on the blue planet?" Great more crazies for my list.

Jeremiah's mouth straight lined. "You're still alive. That's what's important."

Sadie didn't like the direction of this conversation. It was like being trapped inside a run-away car with no brakes, heading straight for a cliff. This really wasn't what she needed right now, but her life did that to her. Her world wasn't at all like the picture perfect place her cover-girl smile implied. She kept getting what she didn't want over and over again. Her gut twisted.

"The way I see it, if you help us stop Bakari al-Sharif you not only protect the world from his insatiable lust for power, you also fix your problem with the KOTL."

"I bite. What's his target?"

"Highclere Castle in England."

She swallowed and took a moment to comprehend. "The Victorian castle where they shoot Downton Abbey?"

"Yes, the home of the eighth Earl of Carnarvon."

"And he has amulets?"

"In 1922, his great, great grandfather, the fifth Earl of Carnarvon, and archaeologist Howard Carter discovered the tomb of Tutankhamen, the boy king of Egypt. In those days archaeologists more or less did what they wanted and the earl took many of the treasures home, feeling justified, as he'd put a lot of time and money into the excavation.

Later his descendants sold most of them to the Met Museum in New York to help pay death taxes, but a few remain on exhibit in the castle. In 1987 more treasure was found in secret cupboards in the walls of the castle.

"So Bakari is after something in the castle?"

Jeremiah nodded. "Two weeks ago a maid found another hidden cubbyhole and made another discovery: a scarab pectoral made of precious jewels, wrapped in an ancient papyrus scroll. The experts believe it belonged to Tutankhamen and it's similar to the one housed in the British Museum, only in better condition. It's official name is *Nebkeheperure* which means, '*Re*, the sun god, is lord of all,'. It's also King Tut's throne name."

"King Tut!!" She stretched her neck to the side. "Oh great. "Let me guess, again. Our friend, the arms dealer, has become obsessed with obtaining it."

"To save his daughter."

Sadie's mouth went dry.

"The Carnavon's are having a gala coming-out party for the scarab. The plan is to hold a ceremony commemorating the handing over of the artifact to the British Museum. They will send it on tour to the world's largest museums." He toggled a key on his keyboard, and a picture of the scarab appeared on the large monitor behind his head, the one he used for briefings.

Sadie leaned forward to get a good look. Truly magnificent. Gold, lapis lazuli, red carnelian and turquoise. A majestic beetle. Fit for a pharaoh. She mused about how odd it seemed for anyone to prize a beetle, but the ancient Egyptians believed them sacred. They believed they held magical protective and healing powers. Of course Bakari would want this. She twisted her neck, trying to clear her head.

Sebastian wouldn't like what she was thinking. *Too bad for him.* She looked at Jeremiah.

He sat expressionless watching her face. She felt like a monkey in a zoo.

"I'll do it," she said.

CHAPTER 9

New York City

*S*adie's sparsely furnished New York apartment had been her home for over a decade. She dropped her bag on the charcoal- gray, leather wing chair by the door and headed straight for the espresso machine in the kitchen area.

Pouring locally roasted coffee beans into the grinder she breathed in their scent as she gave them a good whirl. Minutes later the taste of a perfectly brewed cappuccino revived her spirits.

Being hunted by a religious cult sucked.

On her way to her leather sofa, she picked up the photo sitting on the coffee table. It had a glossy four by five picture of JaJa her son, not by blood or legal adoption, but by heart. He lived in Nigeria with missionaries. She supported him financially and hoped someday to become a larger part of his life. They had had a strange beginning and now he had a large piece of real estate in her heart.

Sebastian had offered to get legal, international, adoption papers drawn up for her, but she told him not to. The boy was better off growing up in his own culture. She took another sip. He cared about what she wanted. She scrunched her mouth. Sebastian, the kindly giant. She loved the man so much her heart ached.

Checking her phone she found a phone message from him and two text messages from her friend Mitchell. Both wanted her to call them. She groaned. Mitch could wait.

Leaning back she looked at her phone. Would Sebastian understand what she'd just done? One way to find out. She punched in his number.

He picked up after the first ring. "Where the hell are you? I went looking for you at the inn and they said you checked out. What the hell Sadie? I deserve better than this. Does our relationship mean so little to you?"

She swallowed. "Sebastian, we need to talk."

"Yeah?"

"I mean really talk, but not now, not over the phone."

He made a low grumble that resembled the sound of a motor chugging but not really starting.

"Sebastian, I love you. With all my heart I love you. As I have loved no other. You mean the world to me... but sometimes..."

"Sometimes?" Pain wrinkled the edges of his voice.

Sweet Jesus. Hearing his pain ripped at her heart, but she had to say her piece. "I feel smothered. I have to be me."

"What exactly are you saying?"

"I'm in New York. I just got in from seeing Jeremiah. I'm going undercover for the CIA, whether you like it or not." She swallowed. "I'll take down Bakari al-Sharif once and for all."

"Fuck."

"I could use support."

"Fuckin' hell Sadie. I love you. I don't want you to go after that *geiten neuker*."

Goat fucker. Lovely. Now he was swearing in Dutch. She sighed.

"*Mijn liefje* I don't want you hurt."

"My stubborn Frisian," she said but in a tender voice. Sebastian was not just a large man physically, but also in spirit, larger than life. His people came from the north of Holland where only the strong survived. Sometimes—no, most of the time—he acted like a transported warrior from a by-gone era, with a strong set of beliefs and a conquering air.

"I just want you safe."

"And beside you," she said.

"Always, beside me."

"Sebastian, after I take care of al-Sharif we can talk about this."

Silence. Ouch. Sebastian usually rambled. Where was his ramble?

Her hand holding the cell trembled. "Sebastian?"

"You don't have to be so damned independent. You'll get yourself killed if you go after guys like him. Let someone else do it."

"I know what I'm doing."

"Do you?" He growled. "If you go after that orifice..."

Oh shit. "Don't give me an ultimatum, Sebastian, I can't..."

"If you loved me as you say you do, you'd walk away from this. Screw the CIA. Be with me."

"Sebastian, I can't let al-Sharif steal treasure. I have a relationship with him that I can work. The CIA needs me on this."

The phone went quiet for a minute. Then he said, "You know how to reach me. I don't want to talk until you're ready to listen."

The phone clicked off. She looked at it in her hand. A single tear ran down her cheek.

She breathed in, breathed out. He'd come around. He had to.

The Frisian Oath of Allegiance he'd stuck on the wall of his apartment came to her mind: "With five weapons shall we keep our land, with sword and with shield, with spade and with fork and with spear, out with the ebb, up with the flood to fight day and night against the North King and against the wild Viking, that all Frisians may be free, the born and the unborn, so long as the wind from the clouds shall blow and the world shall stand." Every inch of Sebastian Wilde was stubborn Frisian.

CHAPTER 10

Cairo

*B*akari hadn't slept for over twenty-four hours. Wearing black silk pajamas, he'd locked himself away in his office on the main floor of his three-century-old Cairo palace to consider his options. He did his best thinking when no one else was around. For the last eight hours he'd paced the finely woven Arabic rug in his bare feet, its plush texture registering on his skin but not his brain. It remained ransomed by the devil in its own private hell.

In the center of the room, a neatly piled stack of paper sat on a six-foot-long polished mahogany desk waiting for attention, along with his Waterman pen, a gift from Rashida. He'd closed the bullet-proof curtains blocking the light of the sun and the rest of the world. While crystal chandeliers lit most of his home, this room had modern LED lighting in the ceiling and the walls, which he'd turned low so that the space looked muted, like a series of layered shadows at dusk. No music played over the speakers. The only sound in the room was the rumble of his empty stomach. He reached the wall, turned, and paced back again.

How could he help his son? He'd always wanted a son. But this young man was so conflicted and so dangerous. Could Djeserit's prophecy be true? Was he doomed to be an evil sorcerer? No. He was his son. It didn't matter how many times he turned this idea around in his head it didn't fit any sense of reality. Khalid was born of his blood. He'd help him. Somehow.

The sound of the door lock releasing caught his attention. His brother Chasisi entered with his slow limp, shaking his head as if to tell Bakari he could have left the door open. Had he knocked on the door? Bakari couldn't remember hearing anything. Damn, he hated being so distracted.

Chas, born with one leg longer than the other, moved slowly towards him. They embraced the way men do, hard and strong. Then they sat, Bakari behind his desk and Chasisi opposite in a wooden chair.

A maid in a well-pressed uniform scurried into the room with a tray of tea and biscuits. Chas must have ordered this. She placed it on the edge of Bakari's desk. Neither man acknowledged her. Without a word she turned and left the room, her head bent and looking at the floor.

"Welcome back, brother," Chasisi said.

The sound of his familiar voice warmed Bakari. He pushed the button to open the window curtains, to take a good look at him. Blinding Egyptian sunlight streamed into the room.

Chasisi wore a white robe and looked more like a poor merchant from the street market than a rich criminal. Like a chameleon, he had the ability to blend well into any environment and learn its secrets. This skill had been a great asset to the family business. He'd been head of security for the last ten years and Bakari had lost count of the number of times Chas had stopped assassination attempts on his life. His brother listened in places where walls didn't have ears, knew all the comings and goings of the underworld, learned who to trust and whom not to trust. For the last week he'd been scouting out a new deal in Syria. He hadn't shaved in a week. Removing his aviator sunglasses, he revealed bloodshot eyes.

"It's not like you to stay locked away for so long." Chas's tone deepened. "What's wrong?"

Where to start? Bakari sighed. "I met my son."

Chasisi nodded. He took out a package of his filthy cigarillos from his pocket, pulled one out and lit it.

"He..." Bakari scratched his chin. "I..." He leaned back in his chair. "Where do I begin?"

"I warned you his surroundings were decrepit."

Bakari nodded. "Khalid doesn't look like a teenager."

"Ah, so that's what bothers you. What would you expect of a boy who's been raised by a crazy witch in Amsterdam, who thought she could rule the world with an ivory wand."

"He has our eyes and our chin." The warmth of pride spread over Bakari's face. The family resemblance was unmistakable. The young man was an al-Sharif, even if he didn't have the name legally. "And he has Djeserit's soft, cocoa-colored skin. But you know all this. You found him for me." Bakari waved his hand in the air dismissing his own words.

"So what's bothering you?"

"He's ruled by anger and that worries me."

Chasisi tilted his head. "Why? You were once an angry young man, as was I. It's part of growing up. You come of age, look around and don't like what you see. You rail against it and do your best to change it. Then the day comes when you realize that you are—"it"—and you laugh at the process. Give him time Bakari. He's not much more than a child."

"A child with power."

"Power? What power? Surely you're not talking about tarot reading."

"Yes, he can read cards and people. He can see the future like his mother."

Chasisi whacked his forehead with the palm of his hand and grunted. "Bakari, be serious. Djeserit played you. She lived off your belief in her. Don't let your son perpetuate those crazy old ideas in your head. You are too much a man of the world, too much a business man, to let these ideas rule you. Don't let people fuck with your head."

Bakari tried to smile but couldn't hold it in place. No matter how many times he told his brother how accurate Djeserit's prophecies had been, Chasisi refused to believe in them. He claimed it was luck at best. Chasisi may have been the wise one in the family, but he refused to see anything beyond the concrete. How wise was that in the end? "Trust me," Bakari said. "I'm careful about who I allow in my head. Khalid has agreed to come here for a visit and you can see for yourself. The young man is formidable, and ..."

"And what?" Chas blew a perfectly round smoke ring. It drifted in the air, leaving a skunky smell.

Bakari wanted to say "scary," but he refused to fear any mortal man, let alone his own son. Still, when he dealt with Khalid, he dealt with powers beyond the earthly realm. Bakari could manipulate any man, bend them to his will, but spirits from another plane were another matter. "Different," he said. His throat constricted. "Very different."

Chas muttered in street Arabic and leaned forward. " You look like hell. Is there something I can do for you?"

Bakari stood up, unable to sit one minute longer. Raw emotions played havoc in his head. He started pacing. "The bottom line is Rashida is getting sick again. I can't stand by and watch her die."

Color drained from Chas's face. "Bakari, if it is her time, you must let her go. Find peace with the will of Allah."

"Not Rashida. I can't lose Rashida." His fists balled. He'd faced many roadblocks in his life, many disasters, many heartaches, but none came near to causing the pain and anguish in his heart as the mere thought of living without his daughter.

"More amulets? Do you want me to find you more amulets?" Chasisi's voice softened.

Outside the midday sun scorched the earth. Its rays flooded the room, but neither man took notice. Bakari paced the length of the office twice more, then stopped in front of Chas. He looked him in the eye. "Tutankhamen's scarab will be put in the public eye next month. I must have it."

"Just tell me where, and it shall be done."

CHAPTER 11

After talking with *Sebastian*, Sadie took a long, hot shower, her cure-all for the gnarly aches and pains of life. But her sorrow cut deep. The thought of not seeing Sebastian again, not hearing his big laugh, not seeing his wide honest smile, not sharing stories about their every-day lives—not feeling his strong arms around her—hurt. Hurt like hell. She rubbed at the ache gathering in the center of her forehead.

The only thing worse than breaking up would be delaying the process of break-up. Their finale seemed inevitable. Might as well get it over with. She tried to swallow, but the enormous lump in her throat kept getting in the way. Her eyes welled up.

She needed to look at this with a clear mind. It would be better to end their relationship now, before they got in any deeper. It wasn't fair to either of them to prolong the pain if their end was unavoidable. *Sweet Jesus, life sucks.* What was the famous line? "Better to have loved and lost, than never to have loved at all." That sure as hell didn't fit. The love she shared with Sebastian had transformed her life, transformed her.

She put her head directly under the stream of steaming water. Wise spooks avoided long term relationships or, if they had them, kept them within their own community. It made practical sense. Lovers aren't supposed to disappear for long periods of time without explanation and reappear with a coating of lies. Deception ruins trust and eats away at the foundations of true commitment. No one wants to live with sordid lies.

It would be like trying to stand on molten lava. Maybe he would put up with it at first, but sooner or later he'd opt out. How could she expect him not to?

They'd had a hot—that is a very hot—affair for six months, but that was only because she hadn't been taking assignments from the CIA. Now...

As much as she wanted to, she couldn't avoid facing this moment. Being a spook was in her DNA. She rocked it. Knowing her high cheekbones were being put to good use made her feel... worthy in a way she had never felt before becoming a spy.

Her fame opened doors that others could not enter. She was really good at sliding silently through them to do the bidding of her country. What she loved most was the thrill of outsmarting the bad guys. It was better than any chess game.

A shrink in Langley said her dedication was understandable. It had to do with her need to set things right. He said growing up neglected by a single, alcoholic mom had left her with a sense of neediness and helplessness she'd never be able to shake. While she couldn't fix her mom who had died in a car accident ten years ago, she could do her part to fix the world. Doing so, or at least trying to, became more than a vocation. It was an obsession.

It didn't matter if the shrink's ideas about her motivation were right. He got the obsessed part. Espionage gave her energy. Living on the edge super-charged her. As much as she loved Sebastian, she couldn't leave the life.

Well, maybe when she turned sixty. She shook her head. No, not even then. An image of a wily Miss. Marple knitting in the corner of the parlor came to mind. She was a spy.

She toweled off and threw on a well-worn, rose colored robe. Picking up her phone, she went to the bank of windows on the east side of the apartment and looked down at the mid-Manhattan scene. The craziness of life in one of the biggest cities of the world humbled her, cutting her problems down to size. Things would turn out all right. They usually did.

But would "all-right" include Sebastian this time? Her gut wrenched. She had to put him out of her mind, at least, if not her heart, and get operation Anubis underway.

Tapping a number by heart into the cell-phone Jeremiah had given her, she hesitated on the last digit. She needed to get her thoughts organized, her intentions clear, for this conversation. The woman she was calling was closely associated with al-Sharif. She knew her as Eboni.

Sadie had met her six months ago and their relationship was more than a little complicated.

Eboni had been the flight attendant on Bakari's private jet and they had gotten to know each other over a bottle of Chardonnay on a four-hour flight between Amsterdam and Cairo. Sadie plied her for information and while she didn't get much out of her at the time, she felt they bonded over the issue of abused women.

When Sadie disembarked from the plane, Eboni slipped her this phone number. Later that night, she'd reappeared in her bedroom and offered Sadie comfort in any way she chose. Sadie hadn't expected that and, being straight, declined the sexual advance. Bakari, she learned, liked to watch women make love and then join them. Her relationship with Eboni became even more complicated when she saw her at the Met Museum during Bakari's heist. Saw her with stolen goods.

Had Sadie made a real connection with the woman? Only one way to find out.

Sadie pushed the last digit and waited. The phone rang once, then the connection opened. A woman's sultry voice said, "Hello."

"Is this Eboni?"

"Yes. Who's this?"

Sadie closed her eyes and imagined the young Egyptian woman with Cleopatra eyes. "It's Sadie," she said, knowing her number was blocked.

Silence.

"I hope you're well?" A silly question. She needed to move things on, before the woman disconnected.

"I cannot help you," Eboni said. No sadness in her voice, no regret, just certainty.

"I saw you that day in New York."

Silence.

"I know Bakari is planning to steal another relic."

Silence.

At least she hadn't hung up. "Eboni, people treasure ancient Egyptian amulets. And while I agree Americans have no right to keep them, we do display them for the world to see. They are safer here than in your own homeland. Someday I hope they'll be returned. But not until we know they'll be safe."

"Bakari doesn't share his plans with me. I'm sorry I cannot be of any assistance to you."

"Has he left for England?"

She didn't answer right away. Asking her for any information was a long shot. Bakari paid the woman handsomely for the work he did for him, and she was well aware of the dangers of crossing him. Sadie counted on that fragile bond they'd formed talking on the plane when they first met. Counted on her ability to read people. She'd sensed Eboni had had enough of Bakari's violence and was ready to sever ties with him. The line went quiet and then Eboni said, "Sometime next week."

And there it was. Her first lead. How do you say thank you to someone who just risked her life to give you information. "Be safe," Sadie said. "May Allah be with you."

Eboni clicked off.

Next? Sadie phoned Langley and had them check commercial flights between Cairo and London, in case he chose to go that route. He could fly his own jet and she had some ideas about where that would land. There were no legal reasons to detain him. What could she do?

Pacing the small floor of her loft she thought about her target. The man was violent and volatile, a volcano ready to erupt at any provocation, sitting at the helm of the world's largest arms-dealing empire. How could she worm herself into his life this time?

Bakari liked her. Srike that, he *really* liked her. Did she want to play that card?

If she offered to meet with him, he might agree. She paced some more. She'd been ready to sleep with the man before for information. Could she get into that head space again?

Putting on a fresh pot of coffee, she checked her messages. Still nothing from Sebastian.

An hour later, after she'd drained the entire pot, she picked up her cell-phone again. Jeremiah confirmed in a text message that Bakari had a ticket to London on Sunday. She scrunched up her face. Time to take another step. She punched in the number Bakari had given her six months ago.

It rang once.

Bakari al-Sharif answered in his low, rumbling, don't-fuck-with-me-EVER voice. "Yes"

"It's me." She winced imagining the square-shaped lion of a man on the other end of the connection. In his early fifties, and at the top of his violent empire, he suffered no fools or liars. "Sadie Stewart."

Without missing a beat, he replied, "How very nice to hear from you."

"How is Rashida?"

After a moment's hesitation, he replied, "She's not..." The connection went quiet for a full second. "Her doctors tell me the cancer is back and growing fast, but you know that don't you."

"Yes and I'm sorry."

"What do you want from me, Sadie?" So matter-of-fact.

"I'm not quite sure how to say it." She made her voice tremble. "I want to see you."

"Are you playing me?" He laughed. "I thought you were smarter than that."

"My boyfriend just threw me aside." Not entirely true, but not untrue either. The best kind of lie. "And I need to take my mind off the bastard. I thought of you."

"Why me?"

Sheesh, he wasn't making this easy. Most men would take the comment straight to their ego and feel proud but Bakari with his enormous balls of steel, flipped right into suspicion. "I could say it was your money. I could say it was your power. I could say it was your charm. All true a bit, I guess. But what really draws me to you... is your heart."

Had she read him right? Would he take the bait? The secret to being a good liar was to skim as close to the truth as possible. His devotion to his daughter did impress her. She concentrated on her breathing and waited for his response.

"Come to me in Cairo."

Sweet Jesus, she hadn't expected that answer. Wait a minute. Wasn't he supposed to be heading for London? Her heart jumped into her throat and it felt wider than a loaded semi-trailer. Back up would be next to useless in Egypt. As soon as she landed in his country he'd have her, to do whatever he wanted. Gritting her teeth, she looked at the ceiling. What to do?

Someone had to stop him from grabbing another amulet. Was he testing her? "That's a long way."

He chuckled softly. "Sadie, where are you?"

"New York."

"I have some business to attend to. Let me call you back and we'll make plans."

"Soon?"

"Let me look at my agenda and see what I can do."

She laughed. "I'm not used to men *tabling* me."

"Some things *habibti* are worth waiting for."

"So you're going to keep me waiting?"

He laughed. "Americans. You want everything now."

Like there's a better time? "Bakari don't you want me, now? My apartment in New York is very private and if you really want to, you can post a guard in the hallway."

The silence bore a heaviness that was clear even over a cell-phone. "I'll call you."

CHAPTER 12

Cairo

*K**halid Badru researched* his father on the Internet. He asked around about him too, but none of the information he dug up prepared him for walking into the family home in Cairo. Luxury beyond imagination and it made Khalid's skin crawl.

It wasn't like any home he had ever seen. It looked more like a movie set for an epic drama.

How the fuck could Bakari think I'd ever belong here? A centuries old castle made of stone and marble surrounded by lush gardens. *What the hell am I doing here?*

Guided by a servant dressed in a humble white cotton robe, Khalid walked down a long hallway to his father's office. On the walls hung expensive paintings, a Monet, Picasso, and Van Gogh ... Enormous bouquets of flowers sat on antique tables. *Surreal, so surreal.*

Goosebumps rose on his arms and he wished he had some weed on him. He took a deep breath and took in as much of his surroundings as he could. Especially the exits.

He'd seen inside his father's mind. The old man was capable of many things. He could put him son in prison or even kill him, if it suited his purpose. Ruthless didn't begin to explain that man's thoughts.

At the end of the hallway Khalid glimpsed a tall wispy woman dressed in a long brown dress. Her long black hair tumbled down to her tiny waist. Her oval shaped brown eyes looked at him and widened. She nodded before disappearing into a doorway. A nod? What the hell did that mean in Egypt?

His guide suddenly stopped. They'd come to an open twelve foot doorway. Inside, his father sitting behind an enormous mahogany desk waved him in.

"Come in, come in." Bakari said as he rose and moved out from behind the desk. He walked towards the younger man with open arms.

Khalid stilled a shudder as he looked into his father's cold eyes and even colder heart.

He walked towards him slowly, taking in his surroundings with a glance. The room didn't fit with the whole ancient-castle theme that surrounded it. It was a modern space with LED lighting, soft leather and dark, wooden furniture. Bookshelves, filled with old, hardbound books, lined two walls. Floor-to-ceiling windows looked out over a lush garden. The hot desert sunlight streamed in, along with the sound of song birds.

They met in the middle of the office for an awkward moment. Bakari reached out to hug his son. Khalid thrust out his hand. They shook and each smiled in their own way. Bakari gave a wide, confident grin. Khalid's less warm.

Khalid had intended on visiting Bakari in Egypt, but wasn't in a hurry to do so. He did have a life, after all. But last night he had been lured by a pretty face, then grabbed by three men dressed in black, with a limited vocabulary, no deodorant and strong arms. The experience robbed him of any warm feelings about this homecoming event.

His father's handshake had been firm. The stupid old man didn't know enough to be scared. Yet. No one could treat him the way he had.

Bakari motioned to the leather chair opposite his desk. "If you don't feel comfortable calling me father, you can call me Bakari for now."

Khalid sat.

Bakari walked around the polished table and sat in a tall office chair that must have cost the GNP of a small country. "I'm so very glad to have you visit us in Cairo. It's time for you to meet the family, become one of us."

"Like I have a choice?"

Bakari smiled. "You were thinking of coming." He shrugged. "I like to make things happen. So I sent for you. I asked the men to make sure you had a good time before they abducted you."

Khalid smiled, remembering how willing the young woman with the brown hair and freckles had been, willing and skilled. She had moves he'd never heard of, let alone experienced. But he should have suspected something wasn't right. "How much did she cost?"

His father shook his head. "We can afford it."

Khalid scowled. "I don't have to pay for it."

"I didn't mean to hurt your pride, my son. Sometimes paying for it makes it more interesting. Fewer complications and no commitment. I think you'll find it's somewhat addictive. Any woman, any time, willing to do whatever you want. Skilled courtesans from around the world with abilities that will amaze you. You are young. Enjoy yourself. Indulge."

This wasn't the father-son chat Khalid expected. "You're telling me to get laid. A lot."

"Yes. Sex clears the mind. When your body's satisfied you can get things done."

"I like your logic."

"We are men."

"Powerful men. But I have no intention of becoming beholden to you."

"Then consider your time with the whore a small thank-you present. I appreciate your help locating Tutankhamen's scarab. I have made plans to attain it. Now it's time to get to know one another."

"You had your henchmen kidnap me." Khalid's face heated.

Bakari moved his head from side to side. "I wanted to see you."

"Unbelievable. You've gotten so used to having power you think nothing of taking it from others."

Bakari shrugged.

Khalid firmed his jaw. "I've wondered who my father was all my life. I never expected someone like you."

"I hope you make yourself comfortable. Adio, the man who showed you in will see to your luggage. If there's anything you need while you stay here, you can ask him. He's been with our family for twenty-years." He folded his hands on his desk. "Or me."

"I hope you don't plan to control me." *Because that would be really stupid.*

"No." A flash of light crossed his eyes. Anger? Perhaps. It came out of nowhere faster than lightning.

Khalid scanned the room once more and forced his body to relax. The smell of the vase of freshly cut flowers sitting on his desk mingled with stale Turkish coffee.

"You're not used to being part of a large family. You have five sisters, three step-mothers and three uncles. It will take time to get to know everyone and find your place."

"My place, old man?" *I fucking well know my place.*

"A figure of speech."

"Let's get a few things straight. You and I both know I have powers that you want to use. Whether I let you remains to be seen."

Bakari smiled. "You think I want to use you?"

"Yes."

Bakari leaned back, stretched his hands in the air, then clasped them behind his head. His movements appeared relaxed and casual, but Khalid could read his heart, and it remained as black and cold as the devil's, and perhaps even more calculating. "Khalid, it's more complicated than that. Ultimately we all use each other, even those we love. It's the way of the world. Right now I want you to settle into the idea of being part of the family. Then we'll talk about what you want out of life. We have enough power, money and love in this family to take care of everyone's needs."

"What I want?"

"Yes."

"Power, like you."

His smile waned. "Did Djeserit tell you that my power came at a great cost?"

"My mother raised me in Amsterdam and told me not to worry about who my father was, that she'd used him to create me. She said my destiny would be to use my gifts to help others. Those who are blessed with plenty must give plenty." He swallowed. "Or some such crap. She never spoke to me of you."

"Did she teach you...?"

"The old ways? Yes, at first she did, but by the time I turned twelve I grew more powerful than her and started learning on my own."

Sweat beaded Bakari's forehead. "Surely that's not possible."

Khalid closed his eyes and focused energy on the half-filled cup of coffee sitting in front of him. It vibrated, then exploded. Shards of glass flew into the air and liquid spilled on to the shiny desk top. "It's possible."

Without even blinking Bakari reached for tissues to clean the mess. "And what exactly do you want to do with the power you seek?"

"I will become the greatest sorcerer this world has ever known. I will take whatever I want. I will do whatever I want. I will be the most powerful man in the world."

Silence filled the room. Bakari stared at him and sighed. "Is that why you murdered your mother?"

Khalid leaned back. "Not exactly. She caused her own death. She kept pestering me. Wouldn't let up. Do this... Do that... She didn't understand I needed to go my own way, have my own friends, make my own magic."

"What happened?" Bakari leaned forward.

"I performed a ritual to gain the essence of her pure soul. I didn't want to hurt her, I just wanted to tap her power."

"And the ritual killed her?"

The memory of the look in his dying mother's eyes grabbed at Khalid. His face tightened and he looked at the ceiling to gain control. Her look of betrayal mixed with the look of fathomless, maternal love haunted him. He shook his head. "She resisted the spell. I underestimated her strength and, in the end she bested me by choosing to die rather than give me what I wanted."

"Power looks great from the outside, my son, but it's a bitch on the inside. Take my word for it. Power withers all that is good in us. You have made a mistake." He narrowed his eyes. "But your mother forgave you and I forgive you. You must find a way to forgive yourself."

"Fucking platitudes from you?" Khalid's voice rose, though he hadn't intended it to. "Even you know mere forgiveness is not enough. I went too far.

I broke the natural order and I will pay for it. The universe will have her revenge with my misery and ultimately with my blood and soul."

Bakari raised his hand ready to argue.

Khalid shook his head. "No, Father, I know I am a damned soul and I have come to terms with that. It gives me a sense of freedom normal people never experience. I will do whatever I want in this life and not worry about the consequences, because I know my future. I am a damned man."

"But then?"

"I have allies in Dual, the after-world. I will find a place in the darkness, but first I will live a long and wonderful life here on earth."

"Son..."

"You don't get it. I am not like other mortals. I never belonged in the light."

Bakari folded his hands on his desk. His eyes sagged with weariness. "I'm told we all start in the light, but who am I to judge you. Is there nothing I can do to change your mind? You need time to grieve the loss of your mother. Don't rush down a dark path before you know what else there is for you."

"Darkness, father, there is only darkness, for you and for me."

Bakari stared towards the door and Khalid turned to see who was there. The woman in the brown dress.

"Rashida?" Bakari said.

Ah, so this is my half-sister, the one Bakari cannot let die.

CHAPTER 13

New York

*A*s the warm, rosy glow of the
pre-dawn light filtered through the morning clouds,
Sadie finished her third cup of strong coffee. A loud
knocking at the door caught her attention. Who
would want to see her this early? She picked up her
gun from the drawer of her entrance table and
peered through the security hole. In the hallway
stood a short woman in a fuzzy, pink floral
housecoat. Old-fashioned, bristle curlers held her
hair up in a haphazard pattern. Her wide mouth
puckered chubby checks. Reading glasses perched
on the end of her slender nose. Her serious
expression made Sadie wonder. Was she seriously
pissed-off or just plain crazy.

   "Who's there?" called out Sadie.

   "I moved in next door. My name is Beatrice"
When Sadie didn't say anything, the woman

continued. "I saw you enter your apartment yesterday and I wanted to warn you."

"About what?"

"Bob."

"Bob?"

"That's what I thought. You're another stupid broad in New York." She put her hands on her hips and gave an exaggerated sigh. "Honey, you don't have a clue. The supe told me you're an international model who flies all over the place. I thought you might not know what you've come home to." She spoke fast and her words held the unmistakable accent of a well-worn New Yorker.

A nosy neighbor. Sadie clicked the electronic security system off, and undid the five state-of-the-art locks to crack open the door. She left the safety chain in place. The woman's eyebrows furrowed.

"Bob?" asked Sadie. "Tell me about Bob."

"Category two hurricane coming up from the Caribbean. They don't expect it to hit our coast, but no one trusts the weather men. Assholes! They neva get it right."

"So this storm will get worse."

"Yeah. Eighty five to ninety five mile an hour winds and a lot a rain. Don't you gotta a TV?"

"Storm surges?"

The woman's small shoulders shrugged. "The men in suits say not to worry."

Sadie gave a nod of commiseration. Memories of Hurricane Sandy and the storm surge that took out a good part of Manhattan were still fresh in every New Yorker's mind. "I'll turn on the news. Thanks."

The woman tried to look into the sliver of space Sadie had opened, but Sadie's body blocked her view. She gave her a suspicious look, then turned and padded with her fluffy blue slippers down the linoleum hallway.

Sadie made mental notes. Beatrice's back was hunched. Possibly osteoporosis. Five foot six. Mid-sixties, white skin with age spots, died blond hair. She smelled of dish detergent, the generic, lemon brand, and peppermint candies.

Jeremiah could give her a detailed report on the woman within the hour. Why hadn't he told her about Bob? She screwed up her face. Because he would have assumed she knew. God damn it, she'd had her head so buried in her own life she'd almost missed a hurricane. Friggin' hell. Was the woman with the blue slippers a good Samaritan? In New York City? Maybe.

Her gut told her Beatrice was okay, but she'd have the woman checked out anyway. Reaching for her cell-phone, which sat on the entrance table, she wondered if that would be the way her life would end. She'd be worrying about something at the end of her nose and nature would take her out with a hurricane or earthquake. She didn't have time for Bob.

Jeremiah answered her call. "Mornin, sugar."

"I need a new neighbor checked out. She says her name is Beatrice." She gave him the woman's description.

"Got it. Anything else? Have you heard back from Bakari?"

"Not yet."

"Hang tight. I'll get back to you."

He clicked off.

She sent a message to Mitch. The last time New York was hit, the tidal surge swept over lower and mid-Manhattan causing millions of dollars of damage. The flooding brought the busy life of the city to a halt. Politicians immediately pointed fingers at one another trying to shift blame. Precautions against such storms were supposed to have been built, but crucial funds had been reallocated to pet projects... The usual bullshit. Meanwhile, New Yorkers suffered.

Mitch's response: "Thought you knew about Bob. The worst of it won't hit for a few hours. You'll be fine. See you soon."

Turning on her radio to follow the news, she logged on to her lap top. Satellite imagery placed the storm a hundred miles south of the city and about fifty miles off shore. As Beatrice had said, it had swirled its way up from the Caribbean and hit Cuba hard. It picked up speed, but luckily had stayed off the US coast. The weather men kept reassuring their audience that New York would only get a bad rain storm.

Being on the fourth floor of her building, she'd be spared the mess of any flooding. Mitch was right. She'd be okay if she stayed put. But if Bob decided to make landfall, there would be no escaping the chaos of the city. She could drive inland or fly out. That would keep her personally safe, but seriously mess with her plans to see Bakari. Surely he'd phone soon.

Sadie made herself a big mug of Bengal Spice herbal tea and sat in front of her lap top at the kitchen table. She scrolled through new documents from Jeremiah. Bakari's arms business had been very busy in the last six months. Two new contracts and four beheadings.

CHAPTER 14

Cairo

After being dismissed by his
father, Khalid spent the afternoon exploring the
estate. Every inch of the castle had been restored.
Thick Arabian carpets, tapestries, polished wood,
crystal chandeliers, fine furnishings... and not a
speck of dust. Room after room shone with an
opulence that spoke of big money spent with taste. If
the school yard bullies who had teased him about
being a bastard could see him now, they'd choke.

Someday he'd live this well. Fuck that—he
would live even better.

Tonight, at a formal sit down dinner, he'd
meet the family. That was Bakari's plan. They'd
probably disapprove of a newcomer who'd share
their wealth, especially one whose mother had not
been married into the family and had made a living
reading Tarot cards. Oh well, they'd have to get used
to it. His father wasn't the kind of man who would

accept open rifts in his family. No. He was a dictator who expected everyone to cower in his presence and bend to his will.

Khalid wandered outside to feel the Egyptian sun on his skin. Its intensity sizzled.

"You shouldn't be out in the mid-day sun." A soft woman's voice came from behind him. He turned. Rashida his half-sister stood there. Her brown dress hung loose on her frail body, but her voice and spirit were strong.

"I wanted to feel it for a minute."

"I've been to London and Paris, but never Amsterdam." The sweet innocence in her voice soothed him and he hadn't been aware he needed soothing.

Sunshine caught in her thick, raven-black hair which fell loose in waves to her waist, making it shimmer with light, giving her an ethereal look. Dark brown eyes dominated her narrow face with warmth and... kindness; but the dark circles beneath them spoke of the pain and wasting away of life energy within her.

As he looked into her eyes he trembled, sensing the agony of her treatments and the nearness of her death. The way she looked back at him, with such openness, jolted his awareness. He thought for a moment she knew he'd seen inside her and that it was okay with her. She had that calmness people near death develop: an acceptance of what is and what is to come.

He gave her my best smile, though he knew it looked lopsided and goofy. "It's different in Europe," he said. Despite their differences he couldn't ignore a niggling sense of connection. One that grabbed at his heart. He wriggled his nose, recognizing that he wasn't as immune from sentiment as he wanted to be.

"I'm hoping you'll tell me about it, brother." She opened her hand to him beckoning him to come closer.

Khalid blinked when she called him brother, then took her hand. It felt tiny inside his, like a child's. She led him down a narrow path to a bench in the garden, under a flower laden arbor. The air smelled of fragrant flowers and song birds sang pretty songs. The sounds and smells of nature calmed him.

"Tell me about yourself." Her eyes skittered across his face like butterfly kisses.

"I was born in Amsterdam. My mother raised me."

"Is it true she was wise in the old ways?"

Khalid heard her question in his mind before she spoke any words, so he was prepared with an answer. "What some people call sorcery, others call knowledge."

She nodded, her eyes wide.

"Have you ever had your Tarot read?" He had used this line on many young women, and using it on her made him wince. It seemed to cheapen the moment. Still, the words tumbled out. He wanted to impress her.

"Never," she said.

"Never," boomed a man's voice from down the path a few yards away. In long strides a tall Arabic man dressed in a peasant's robe appeared on the trail. Khalid recognized he had the same eyes and chin as his own. Great... more family.

The young man stood to greet the older man.

"Uncle," Rashida began "this is—"

"The son of the whore." Spit flew from the man's mouth as he raged.

"And your blood relative," Khalid said calmly, extending his hand as a peace offering.

The man's two hard, black eyes glared down at him. "You are not my family."

"Bakari thinks differently."

He scowled. "Leave Rashida alone." He reached down and grabbed her by the arm, hard enough to leave bruises.

"Ow!"

Keeping his face as blank as possible, sensing that his hostility could easily erupt into unneeded violence, Khalid looked on. This man had his own crazy set of complexities. *Nothing like being born into a family of weirdoes.*

"What did my mother do to you?"

He froze as surely as if he'd been doused with ice water. Only for a second, but one long enough to speak volumes to the seer's inner ear. There had been a connection between this angry man and his mother and it hadn't ended well for him. He let his face break into a smile. "Was it her power or her body that tempted you?"

"Chasisi, you're hurting my arm." Rashida pushed at the older man's chest.

He released her, nodding his apology, then turned to face Khalid. His eyes narrowed and his mind stonewalled him. "Your mother played Bakari. I warned him to be careful around her, but he wouldn't listen."

"You wanted her."

He laughed. "There was a time when every man wanted her. Your mother was beautiful."

"And powerful." Khalid smiled, unable to hide his pride.

"I don't believe in that crap. She manipulated people. And now she's doing it from the grave through you. I don't care if you are Bakari's latest interest. If you do anything to harm this family, I will see to it that you die a nasty death." For an instant he let Khalid slip into his mind, to see that death, the one he intended for him. A short square man with dead-looking eyes stood over his still body holding a hatchet dripping with blood, his blood. Khalid shivered.

"Okay I get it, old man. You're jealous Bakari laid her."

The man's face turned bright red and his hands shook.

"No, uncle, no," said Rashida.

"Relax," Khalid said. "I don't want to hurt my sister. I'd like to get to know her." He looked at her with gentle eyes. "My company is good for her. Being shut-in this place, with only family and servants would drive me crazy."

A muscle in Chasisi's right cheek twitched as Khalid spoke. He looked away scowling.

"Please, uncle."

Chasisi grunted. "No Tarot, no magic, no mumbo-jumbo crap. And watch your language."

"Got it," Khalid said. "I'll tell her stories about pretty European cities and gardens."

The older man raised his brows.

"Selected stories."

"Chasisi," he said, "I am Bakari's younger brother." He offering his hand.

His steel-like grip squished Khalid's fingers, but he didn't flinch. He would never give him that satisfaction.

Chasisi leaned towards his ear and spoke in a hushed tone so that Rashida could not hear. "You harm anyone in our family, and your balls will hang on my wall."

CHAPTER 15

Bakari sat behind his polished desk looking at his son. "How far away can you read a mind?"

"Depends on the mind." Khalid, looking like a reluctant-to-be-breathing teenager, slouched back in the chair opposite his father. The door of the office had been closed and locked. There were only the two of them inside.

The afternoon desert sunlight streamed through the windows, but no fresh air. Everything had been locked up tight. Bakari wanted privacy.

"There is a woman in New York ..."

Khalid laughed. "You're asking for help with your love life?"

"It's more complicated than that. This woman worked for the CIA and we have crossed paths before."

"Does she know about your business?"

Bakari nodded. "I expect she knows everything." He steepled his hands on the desk.

"Does she know about your plans to take Tut's scarab?"

Bakari's mouth firmed. "That could be why she contacted me."

Khalid looked hard at him for a long minute and then away. "I can see her in your thoughts, like an image in a painting. I can't read her there, especially since your feelings for her change who she is in your mind. She is more like a dream than a person. I need to be near her to get a reading."

He closed his eyes for a moment. "I have to ask. If you are so attracted to her, why don't you go fuck her?"

"She's dangerous."

Khalid opened his eyes and smiled. "That's part of her appeal. You wonder if you can truly possess her." He laughed. "But that's something I can't tell you, old man."

Bakari stood and walked to the window. He watched a bird perched on the limb of a tree singing its heart out. "I have had many women in my life, but this one..."

"If you want her in your life, you need to turn her. You know that. You can't risk playing with dangerous women."

"Yes, I need her on my side. But how? Normal women you can woo with flowers, chocolate or jewelry, but not her."

***

Khalid closed his eyes for a moment and focused on the woman. He could see her perched on top of the terrace banister, three stories up from a canal. Venice? Her heart pounded and her eyes were on fire. "The woman loves danger," he said.

Bakari nodded. "I've thought about that. It may be what draws her to me. She knows my life is dangerous. I'm dangerous."

"So lure her with more danger."

"How—"

Khalid raised his hand up to stop his father from saying more. "Let her ride the edge between life and death as much, and as often, as you can. That's what turns her on." He chuckled. "Bring her close to you. Let her feel your true nature. That would scare any mortal woman."

CHAPTER 16

Amsterdam

*B*ack in his office at his art gallery, Eros, in a seventeenth century canal house on Herengracht, Seb worked through the stack of papers his assistant had placed on his desk. Most of them only needed a signature, but they all should be read. Should be... He couldn't make himself focus.

Balling an old memo into a tight sphere, he considered where to throw it. Lobbing it high in the air, he watched as it sailed easily into a pot on a nearby side table. *If life could only be as easy as that throw.*

He'd planned to spend two weeks with Sadie, not to be fucking with accounts. When he decided to start his business five years ago, he had no idea how much paperwork would be involved. Then he became successful and tons of fucking paper fell from the sky like demonic ticker-tape.

The morning sun streamed through the tall window beside his desk, overlooking the canal.

Doves cooed outside, and the smell of fresh coffee wafted up to his room. Paul, his assistant, trying to make him feel better, had spent the morning brewing pot after pot.

Rascal, his Siamese cat with attitude, leaped into his lap,. His steely-blue, cat eyes stared at him through his black mask as he mewed, which sounded like an angry person muttering.

"Demanding brat," Seb said. As he rubbed beneath the cat's chin the babble turned into a purr. The purring grew, lightening Seb's mind for a whole minute. Is this what he'd become—an old man with a cat? An opinionated cat? Rascal purred louder, obviously liking the idea. He had never been fond of Seb's women.

After five minutes of attention, the cat settled on his lap, molding himself to his Sebastian's abdomen. He reached over his long body, grumbling as he signed his name on a sales document.

He shook his head. *I'm getting self-absorbed. I'm moaning over a woman when I should be feeling good about life. My life is good.* Since he was a little kid, he'd loved art. Creating a business buying and selling it was a dream-come-true. He couldn't let himself forget that. He had so much to be grateful for.

Sadies's soft green eyes came to mind. Shit. He had to stop thinking about her. There were other women in the world, ones who wouldn't expect him to change to suit them.

But he didn't want any of them. He threw his pen against the wall. It made a thud when it hit and left a blue ink stain on the fresh white paint. "*Godverdomme.*" Rascal jumped to the floor and strode from the room, his long tail erect. Its end curled and twitched. Great, now he'd pissed off his cat.

Seb grimaced.

The sound of feet padding softly up the creaky narrow stairway caught his attention. Paul with fresh coffee? It would be his fifth cup, though he hadn't drunk more than half of them. He turned to face the door.

A few seconds later, his Tante Zenneke entered. She had a tall lean body. Long, blond hair streaked with gray, fell loosely over her shoulders. Her eyes were Dutch blue and her skin porcelain white. Around her neck hung layers of thick heavy jewelry. She was eccentric as she looked, but he loved her dearly. She was more than an aunt, more like a mother.

He stood to greet her with open arms, then froze on the spot as her expression hit him like a soccer ball between his eyes.

"What's wrong? I thought your doctor said you were okay."

"It's you I'm worried about. What's going on with you and Sadie?" She grabbed the front of his soccer shirt and pulled his head down to kiss him three times on his cheeks, the Dutch way. First one, then the other, then the first again.

Seb returned the kisses then gave her a look that would kill most people. She should know better than to ask about Sadie. If Seb had something to share, he would. But he didn't. At least not yet.

Wait how did she know? He hadn't gotten around to telling her he was back in town, let alone why he'd come home early. Had Xander ratted him out? No, probably his wife. The women talked a lot. He ran a hand through his hair. "Good to see you, Tante Zen."

"I hear you got drunk with Xander last night." Her clear voice held no judgment, just fact.

"I don't want to talk about it?"

"I like Sadie." She glared at him, as if he was a beast.

"I know. I do too." His chest tightened. Did he really have to talk about it?

"Then why are you letting your relationship fall apart?" Her eyes fluttered around the room like a manic dragonfly, taking in every detail. She stopped at the pen mark, sighed, and went on.

"It's not my fault," he said to draw her eyes back to him.

"Men. Just tell me what happened."

"She..." He swallowed. "We..." Where to start? "She's stubborn and too independent for me."

Zenneke cackled. "Look who's talking!"

True, Seb had been called stubborn on occasion, but he didn't see it that way. "I just know my mind. I'm not like her."

"What did she do?"

Silence. He had to tell her something, or she wouldn't leave. "Sadie thinks I'm too clingy."

"So stop the cling." Zenneke opened her hands in the air, as if it were an easy thing to fix.

He scratched his chin. "Tante Zen, I don't want to talk about her."

Her soft, wizened face contorted into a grimace, the one she'd used when he brought home bad report cards from school. "Is Sadie still in Venice? Go to her. Work it out."

"She's in New York." Would this morning ever end?

"New York?" Her eyes flashed wide.

"Yah, the Big Apple."

"Get off your ass and get moving. There's a hurricane off the eastern seaboard. They don't think it will land, but at the very least they will have one hell of a storm." Her eyes twinkled with mischief.

Seb wanted to tell her that Sadie had an umbrella and could take of herself, but when he caught the glint in her eyes he stopped. The storm could be a good excuse to turn up back in Sadie's life. There would be no loss of face in the shadow of a hurricane. They could call it a truce until the gale force winds passed and maybe they would be able to work things out in the meantime. With luck they would lose power and have to sort things out in the dark. A smile broke on his face. He stood up and gave his Tante Zen a big kiss.

CHAPTER 17

New York

*S*adie fell asleep watching the
news on TV, with a bowl of popcorn on her tummy.

Gasping for air, Sadie stood by the small pond surrounded by dense vines and …. The jungle heat and fetid smells of wild vegetation, animals and people surviving on the edge of civilization compressed her lungs. Drums beat in the village a half mile away. Holding the baby in his arms the witch doctor in the vibrant orange and red robe walked to the empty grave chanting to his gods. His words rhythmical and seductive filled her with a heavy sense of dread. She tried to swallow, but couldn't. If only he would stop. If only she could do something to make him stop.

Using vines, the shaman strapped the newborn Ja Ja between the breasts of his dead mother lying on the ground. The grave digger watched without emotion. The shallow grave waited.

"Nooooo," Sadie yelled.

Filled with terror, she awoke and sat up. The bowl of popcorn flew into the air and she grabbed at the popcorn cascading in every direction. *That damn dream again.* Drenched in sweat, she collected her thoughts. She hadn't had the nightmare for six months; not since she'd met Sebastian. Why now? She picked the bowl up from the floor.

Sitting on the coffee table, her cell-phone vibrated. May as well check it. It could be Bakari.

It wasn't him. She sighed. Or Sebastian. It was a text from Mitchell her best friend. He was in town between modeling assignments. Sadie didn't like models as a rule, but Mitch was different.

Most models were supreme bitches, the nasty result of the highly competitive world of fashion in which they lived, fueled with cocaine and booze. They believed that a grotesque sense of beauty was more important than anything else in the world. Not true beauty, of course, but the kind that comes with layers of expensive make-up and puking your body as thin as a clothes hanger. They idolized the ability to keep pouting for cameras.

Mitch was different, a rebel in her world, with a clear head and a big heart. He'd been her best friend for five years, ever since they got drunk in the Alps after a photo shoot that had gone wrong. With finely chiseled features Michelangelo would have drooled over, dominated by big, brooding, brown eyes, people often mistook him for a movie star. He was definitely a fifteen on a ten-point scale of metro-male handsome. She had wanted to jump his bones when she first met him, but soon learned that he preferred his lovers tall, dark and sexy with stubble on their chin.

"Sadie," he wrote, "How's Venice?"

"In NY"

"WTF?"

She smiled. He'd remembered how excited she was about her anniversary plans with Sebastian. She tapped her reply. "Long story."

"I can be there in twenty."

Thirty minutes later he tapped on her door. She opened it and he rushed in to give her a big bear hug. Sometimes that hug was all she needed to feel happy, but not tonight. She poured them both a glass of wine and she told him her story. Mitch knew a bit about her life as a spy, so she didn't have to hold much back. It wasn't usual for a civilian to know so much, but he'd been around her enough to see what was going on in her life.

"So let me get this straight," he said. "Sebastian Wilde, *the Sebastian Wilde*, the seven-foot mouth-watering Viking warrior, dressed as a genie, offers you three erotic wishes and you come running home to the States?"

"It's complicated."

"Woman, I could give him a long list of wishes. That man is so hot, just the thought..." He stopped when she glared at him.

"There's more to life than sex," she said.

Mitchell peered down his nose and crossed his eyes as if that was the craziest thing he'd ever heard. "I didn't get that memo."

"Hmmm.

He studied her face for a moment. "I get what you're saying. This is about more than three..." he paused dramatically, "erotic-dreams come true." His smile turned wicked. "Shake your head darling. The two of you are in love. You both like adventure. You both want to save the world. You're both bat-shit crazy, if you ask me, but that's who you are. You are made for each other."

"But I—"

"Don't blow it. Not for the fucking CIA that treats you like a drone with tits, or for your grand sense of justice, or for... shit, anything. Nothing matters more."

"A drone with tits? I like that one." She started to laugh and the laughter grew deeper until it came from deep in her belly. The image was just too much. He joined in. Her shoulders relaxed and she sank into her sofa, feeling as though the world might just right itself again. The Mitch-effect. No matter how bad life became, he found some way to make her laugh. She punched his arm.

He leaned back in the lounge chair facing her and sighed. "Three wishes..."

"I have to make him understand."

"Good luck with that, darling. He's all male. He wants to protect you, and no matter how many times you tell him you can take care of yourself, he'll keep wanting to be your hero. It's a hard-wired testosterone thing with guys."

"I love being a spook. It's exciting and I get to help our country. Why can't he get that?"

"Why can't you take an easier operation?"

"Someone had to stop the man. He sells guns to child soldiers. Even to the Islamic State." She shuddered. "After I get this guy, I can see about easier assignments."

"You think Sebastian will wait for you."

"Counting on it." He had to. Right? He had to respect her. He had to understand why she had to do this. When you love someone...

"Face the facts, sweetie. Going after that scumbag, again, will rip Sebastian apart. Have you forgotten the guy is one of the most dangerous men in the world? Give your head a shake. Sebastian wants you safe. He wants to protect you. Thinking of you out there, putting yourself in danger, will kill him." Mitch squeezed the bridge of his nose. "And Sweety, screwing the arms dealer takes it to another level. Sebastian will go ape-shit and I don't blame him. He doesn't want you in another man's bed—any other man's bed—let alone this asshole's."

"You're sounding Neanderthal."

"Honey, I'm just calling it as I see it. You're expecting too much from Sebastian. Maybe if he didn't know what you were throwing yourself into, it might work, but he does know. He knows you're fully aware of what you're about to do and that makes it worse. How would you feel if he fucked a woman for his flag?"

"If she stirred up as much evil in the world as Bakari al-Sharif, I'd understand. Sex is just a physical act, after all. I'll think about it like a gymnastic routine with lots of messy fluids."

"With another man." Mitchell's eyes as molten brown as a Labrador puppy's, melted into hers. Damn, he knew how to mess with her head.

"It wouldn't mean anything," she said. But a cold finger ran up her spine.

Mitch winced. "And now we come down to the Mata Hari question. Can you detach yourself enough to have passionate sex with the man, please him in every way he desires to get the information you need, and not have it corrupt you in any way?"

Sadie's lower lip slid between her teeth. She hoped so. Sometimes hope was all a woman had. To date she hadn't screwed anyone for information. Flirted a hell of a lot, but never screwed. She ran a hand through her tangled hair. Bottom line: she believed in doing the greater good. That's what kept her going, helped her navigate the murkiness of that world. "Hell, yeah." She swallowed and added, "I'll fix this. I'll phone Sebastian and explain it all over again. He'll understand. I'll make him understand."

"Good luck with that."

CHAPTER 18

Coffee wasn't enough. Sadie hit her yoga mat. Finishing her last in a series of ten deep Salutations to the Sun, Sadie stopped her yoga in the standing position. Was that a dog barking? She wiped at the sweat on her forehead. Yup, definitely a dog barking. Now scratching? Whose friggin' dog? No one had a dog on her floor. Did they?

As she walked over to her door the barking grew louder. Looking through the spy hole, she saw a young man with a bored expression knocking. After grabbing her gun from the entrance table, she undid her five dead-bolts. Keeping the safety chain in place she opened the door a few inches. "What do you want?"

The man stood about her height, five foot eleven. Okay twelve, but she never admitted that. He wore baggy jeans that hung low on a too-skinny waist. Probably a vegan or a druggie. The smell of cheap male cologne wafted from him. The logo on his white polo shirt read: *Express Man,* and below that was his name: *Randy.* This had to be Mitch's doing. He was trying to lift her spirits with a prank.

The delivery man's green eyes lacked focus. He talked to her door. "Delivery for Sadie Stewart." His accent nailed him as a New Jersey guy.

The sound of barking drew her eyes down to the floor. On the end of a leather leash stood a foot-long ball of fur, bouncing up and down. She jerked her eyes up to the man's. "Not the dog."

"Yeah lady, the dog." His mouth scrunched up and he sighed, as if this was the dumbest delivery he'd ever had. Maybe it was.

"I don't want a dog." *Don't look at it, again.*

"You Sadie Stewart?"

Don't look at the puppy. "Who sent you?" *Don't...*

Slowly, as if the effort was beyond his abilities, he pulled a crumpled piece of paper from his pocket. It looked twenty years old. "No name. Paid cash. No return address." He balled up the paper and pushed it deep into his pocket. "Lady, you *gotta* take the dog."

Her eyes, against her better judgment slid down to the puppy. His big brown eyes melted instantly into hers. *Double friggin' hell.* She needed to nail an Egyptian arms dealer, fix her relationship with her Dutch lover, and fit in a couple of photo shoots in Italy to keep her international modeling cover. She had no time to take care of a dog in New York. But she couldn't tear her eyes from his. He was just too damn cute.

Randy started shuffling from one foot to the other, as if he'd missed his designated potty time.

"Lady, I got other deliveries. I'm an Express Man. That means something in our business. I'm supposed to be fast. Will ya just take the dog and sign for it?" He pushed a handheld device towards her.

Express Man... sign... dog... she got all of that, but... Her eyes stayed with the puppy. She'd never had a puppy. Always wanted a puppy. It would be hers. He had to be the cutest puppy she'd ever seen. He wouldn't argue with her like Sebastian.

Wait. Could he somehow be a threat? She pushed her gun into the waistband of her yoga pants, at the base of her spine, and unhinged the security chain.

When she opened the door she checked the hallway. Clear. Then she bent down to examine the puppy. The dog tried to jump into her arms, and when she put her finger to his mouth he gave her a good chomp with sharp little dagger teeth. This little guy had character.

"Lady?" Randy's right eye twitched as if he'd caught a bug in it.

It would be stupid to take this little beast. Really stupid. He looked like a fluffy little chocolate piglet. She couldn't take a mutt around the world with her on her shoots. She couldn't let him mess up her CIA work. He'd have to have a dog-sitter. His little tongue felt like sandpaper as he licked her arm. His short tail flew back and forth with vigor. She couldn't do this.

Could she? A year ago she'd fought herself over keeping a baby. It made no sense to adopt one, especially since she was single and nomadic. In the end, the decision took less than a heartbeat. She couldn't stand there and watch a newborn baby being put to death. She'd never regretted taking over the care of JaJa, even though she rarely saw him. That had worked out. So why couldn't she adopt a dog? Lots of people did it.

"Ladeeee?"

"What kind of dog is it?"

"It's a puppy."

She rolled her eyes.

"Do I look like a dog expert?" He shrugged. "Listen, lady, if you don't want him I'll throw him down the garbage chute."

And have him compacted? Her gut wrenched and she glared at him. The asshole would probably do it too.

He shrugged again.

The puppy rolled onto his back for a tummy scratch and she complied. He looked a bit like a baby Labrador, but too fluffy to be a purebred. She liked that idea. Her pedigree was far from pure and any animal connected to her should be equally mottled. Not that those things should matter, but having grown up on the other -side -of -the -tracks she had plenty of scar tissue from comments slung at her years ago.

If she chose a dog she'd want him to be big, tough and lovable. This puppy with his oversized paws looked as though he could meet her expectations.

Like Sebastian? Where the hell did that idea come from? Dog. Concentrate on the canine.

"Lady the wind is picking up. Hell of a storm brewin' there. I got things to do."

Wind? What a pussy. There's always wind in New York. Without any more thought, she grabbed the handheld device and signed her name.

Randy gave her a victory smile as he handed her the dog's lead. "He's got the runs, by the way."

CHAPTER 19

The mutt strutted into Sadie's apartment as if he owned it. Then he ran full speed to the other end of the room and tried to stop, but the shiny wooden floors gave him no traction and he slid right into the wall and bounced off of it with a yelp. Sadie giggled. She scooped him up into her arms, retrieved a bug searching device from her kit in her bed side table and took him to the kitchen counter for inspection. She used the two-inch-long device to scan his body, which should have been easy, because he was small, but wasn't because he wouldn't be still. He thought it was a game and kept trying to grab it in his mouth. Reasonably certain he wasn't a bug carrier, at least not of the electronic kind, she took him to the bathtub.

His brown eyes gave her the most plaintive look as she bathed him, in case he was covered in some chemical. Wrapped in a thick towel, he totally forgave her as she rubbed his curly coat dry. Spunky guy. Maybe that should be his name. Nah, he didn't seem like a Spunky. Too regal for that. *How about Monster, because his paws are so large?* Nope. He'd no doubt cause trouble, but she didn't want people to think of him as a disaster waiting to happen. Settling into her big recliner with him wrapped in the wet towel on her lap felt too-right. As she scratched under his ears his tail wagged and tapped lightly on her arm, magically easing the sadness in her heart.

Who ever heard of a spy having a fluffy puppy? Jeremiah would kill her. The thought of his distress pushed the edges of her smile wider, until her whole body was smiling. To hell with the men in her life. Who cares what they or anyone else thinks. She'd enjoy the simple pleasure of a dog. The puppy started to leap up at her, as if he knew she'd crossed a line in the sand.

Wonder if he's hungry? As she fried a steak she considered where the pup came from. Her list wasn't long: Mitch playing a prank that went too far; Sebastian trying to be extra sweet; Bakari making a weird love offering; or some nefarious stranger. *Did the KOTL like dogs?*

Okay, Mitch was definitely capable of devious pranks, so he stayed on top of the list. Maybe she'd call the dog Mitch to spite him.

Sebastian? Giving a dog to a woman in New York, who he wanted to see more of in Amsterdam, didn't make sense, so he had to be struck off the list.

Bakari? Violent wing-nuts who believe themselves to be powerful were unpredictable, but gifting a dog didn't fit his MO either.

Back to Mitchell. Crazy, fun-loving Mitchell.

As the smell of the steak grew stronger the puppy drooled. And drooled. How could one little beast contain so much spit?

When the meat was done, she cut up a quarter of it into small pieces and hand fed him. She'd heard that was a good way to create a bond. He choked the pieces down quickly and eyed her as if to say, "Where's the rest, Mamma?" She laughed and gave him a bit more. Who could resist those chocolate-brown eyes?

Then she left him on the floor wrestling with his soggy towel as if he were a lion and the towel his prey, while she ate her portion and watched the evening news. The hurricane was off-shore. Satellite images showed the swirling storm. The winds were peaking at sixty-five miles an hour. The rain fell in torrents. Trees were bending and breaking. The possibility of another storm surge breaking the banks of the Hudson River and sweeping into Manhattan was mentioned as a side note. *Hate those side notes.*

She washed the dishes as the puppy pulled at her pant leg. Sharp nails dug into her leaving scratches on her skin. Still no word from Bakari or Sebastian. Looked as if she had to ride out the storm with her new little guy. "Ow," she called out as he nipped her skin.

The puppy had to be a gift from Mitch. He was the only person in her life zany enough to think she could manage a dog. As if on cue, she heard a knock on the door.

Mitch marched in with two over flowing bags of stuff and an irresistible smile. "Isn't he cute?" he said.

"Cute," she said as she threw the dog's soggy towel at Mitch's head. "How the hell can I take care of him?"

"You'll work that out." From the top of the first bag he pulled out a rope attached to a ring and wiggled it in front of the dog. "Here, boy," he called. The dog grabbed onto it and began pulling. *Great! Tug of war in my living room.*

"Seriously, Mitch, I'm too busy. You do remember that I fly all over the place."

"Yeah, yeah." He gave me a piercing look. "But, darling, you need to learn how to chill out."

At that precise moment the dog squatted and peed on Mitchell's shiny shoes. Sadie laughed. Mitch's eyes popped and he shook the dog off his foot. Sadie laughed even harder, then Mitch joined in.

Mitch exited for the bathroom to clean himself up, and Sadie grabbed some paper towel from the kitchen. "I hope you brought something to help me train him."

Silence.

"Mitchell? Newspaper, a mat... something?"

He returned without a word and rummaged in his bags, placing all sorts of interesting items on her coffee table. Three chew toys, two boxes of puppy treats, a small piece of rawhide and a book— *How to Raise Your Dog*. Nothing to catch poop. "This book has everything in it and it's all indexed in detail in the back."

"Okay. Does it have a section on peeing on shoes?"

The corners of his mouth twitched. "Sadie, we have to get serious."

This couldn't be good.

"You need to think about what you're doing. You were getting yourself together with Sebastian, but now you're back with the CIA." He spit the letters out like poison. "It's insane. I feel like I'm watching you ride a motorcycle straight into a brick wall. " He exhaled a loudly and at length. "You gotta stop worrying about saving the world and save yourself."

"My life, my decision," she said.

Slowly, he shook his head. "Does this mean you won't keep the dog?"

She firmed her bottom lip. "How can I?"

"We can take turns caring for it, and when we're both out of town I'll get my vet friend, Seymour, to take him. We can do this together. It'll be our own family."

Listening to sophisticated Mitchell beg like a ten-year-old boy with a bad case of puppy-love made her feel warm and fuzzy, despite her worries. "You know that sounds..."

"Good?"

"I'm not ready to say that good, yet. But maybe—possible. *How can I even consider a hound in my life! There's no room.* She drummed her fingers on her arm. Her mind told her one thing, but her heart another. "You'll house train him when I go back to Europe?"

"And I'll send you pictures."

Her heart fluttered. Talk about an offer she couldn't refuse.

"We could call him Mojo," Mitch said.

Sadie laughed. "We could both do with more mojo in our lives." She eyed the fluff ball with the huge paws and big molten eyes. "But, he doesn't look like anything to do with voodoo."

"Fido?"

She grimaced. "Fido doesn't cut it."

He took a crumpled piece of paper from his pocket. "I made a list of names."

"Hoover, Giles, Herbert, Maxwell Smart—I couldn't resist the spy connection—Dossier, Slick, Double O—you know the James Bond thing—Sunny, Revere, Jello, Choco, Artemis, Glock, Sherlock, Snoop, Boris, Nathan, Donovan, Cyrus or Scout?"

Sadie reached for his list. "You've taken your time on this."

"Me and some friends. What do you think?"

A smile slid over her face. "I'm overwhelmed. The little guy is so damn cute. He's irresistible. Let me think on these names. I want to find one that really fits. In the meantime, I'm calling him Puppy."

He nodded.

The windows rattled from the wind. They never rattled, but then she hadn't there for the last blow. "Want to hunker down with me while I wait for a phone call? We can play with Puppy."

The dog had fallen asleep on Mitch's chest. "No, I won't stay. That's another reason I came by. All my photo-shoots have been canceled. I'm heading inland. Want to join me?"

She shook her head. "Can't. I won't even go into why."

Mitch got up and handed her the dog. "Keep in touch."

The puppy squirmed in her arms. His baby dog smell hit her nostrils and she gave him a cuddle. "Aren't you taking him?"

"Not in my new car." With that he left before she could utter another word.

With care, she placed the squirming beast on the floor. His paws spread in every direction at first, then he got his balance and ran in circles. Although she really, really didn't need him in her life, he added something wonderful. She sighed and picked up her cell-phone to check messages.

A distinct odor hit her. She took a good sniff. Was that the smell of...? She looked down at the little guy. He sat at her feet, wagging his tail with glee. Beside him was a pile of poop... on her new ten-thousand dollar floor. She smirked. James Bond never had dog issues.

She was on her hands and knees with paper towel when she heard the key in the first lock. Only two people had keys: the supe and Sebastian. Her chest tightened. Her gut sank then twisted into a tight knot. Placing a handful of poop into a plastic bag with paper towel, she gritted her teeth. She hadn't even showered yet. Her hair had to be a mess. That didn't matter so much. He always made a mess of it when he saw her anyway. An image of them in bed making passionate love sprang into her mind and a hot jolt of lust flowed through every inch of her.

Sebastian entered the apartment without a word. He walked over and stood above her, all six feet five inches of him, and looked down. The poop was off the floor, but the smell hovered in the air. She sprayed the area with a disinfectant and didn't look up.

"A dog?"

The puppy made little barking sounds as if he was a trained watch dog; so squeaky-adorable she wanted to grab him and cuddle him. Her nose twitched. How could anything that cute make such a stinky mess; and how could she not really mind? She wiped the floor with a clean piece of paper then sprayed it again.

With his large hand, Sebastian reached past her and scooped up the plastic bag full of doo doo. "I'll be back."

CHAPTER 20

Seb returned from his doo-doo run to the garbage chute down the hall, washed his hands and sat down in his favorite leather chair in the living room. "I called and sent you text messages a million times."

Sadie sat on the couch opposite. The puppy lounged in her arms, making mewing sounds. They looked good together, like a family. A family, without him? She tilted her chin up the way she always did when she'd determined what her next move was in her mind. No eye contact. Not good. Finally she spoke. "There's nothing left to say."

"Sadie, I love you."

She sighed.

"I can't just let things stop here, like this. We're good together."

"You mean the sex is hot."

"Yeah the sex is hot, but you and I both know it's more than that. Much more."

"Endorphins pop, hormones surge... It's all about the chemistry."

"Fuckin hell Sadie. You know the chemistry runs deeper than that."

"Do I?" She looked at him. Her beautiful moss-green eyes drooped with sadness. "Sebastian, it's not going to work between us. You don't get *me*."

Oh how he wanted to get her, all of her, right now. He'd like to push into her with all his force, fill her up, prove his love to her, and ... He clenched his jaw. "I know you think of yourself as a big, tough spy. I know you can fight better than most soldiers and I know you're good with a gun and a knife. But I also know the other side of you. You are the kindest, gentlest and most loving woman."

Sadie looked away from him towards the rattling windows.

"There is a mystery that is you," he continued. "Part intense sensuality and part deep pain that longs for connection. I want to be that connection. I want to be with you. I..."

Her eyes brimmed with tears.

"In Venice..." His voice trembled. "I wanted to ask you to live with me."

"Sebastian, don't." Her eyes implored him.

"What is it I don't get? Tell me. Give me a chance."

"I need to be free."

What the hell could he say to that? "Fuck." He growled. Honestly, what did she expect of him?

"Stud..."

Oh Shit. I can't believe she's calling me that. Not now. It was a name she called him in the bedroom, or on the couch, or on the table, or in the bathroom on the plane... or... wherever they were making love. Usually just before she came, and she came a lot, long hard orgasms that rocked his world as well as hers. He shuddered thinking about them.

"We've had a good run, especially considering I'm a spook."

"But you don't have to be, *mijn lieftje*." She should come home with him to Amsterdam. They could have a good life together there. Money would never be a problem. He'd make sure of that. Business was good. They could have fun. If she'd only let it happen. He stared at her as hard as he could, trying to convey all he felt, hoping that would be enough.

"Be honest with yourself. You knew we wouldn't last. Not us." She put the puppy on the floor and ran a hand through her beautiful, thick hair. Light reflected along the strands of her auburn curls.

He wanted to touch her.

"Part of you must have known," she continued. "You never stay with one woman for more than a month. We beat your record by five months."

Her matter-of-fact voice scratched at his heart. "But you... We... are different," he said.

"It's for the best. You'll have fun playing around again."

He swallowed. Shit. He hated talking about feelings. "Sadie, I'm not the man you think I am."

Her eyes flashed at him.

"I wanted to tell you before, but it never seemed to be the right time. We were always having so much fun." He swallowed. "If you knew more about me, you wouldn't think me a shallow, good-times guy."

She raised her brows.

"Tante Zen did her best to raise me, but I was a hellion." He hesitated, not sure he wanted to go on. Shit he hated talking about his past. "I was an angry, lost kid. I felt abandoned and couldn't figure out where I belonged. At thirteen I started hanging out with some really bad people. They made me feel okay about myself."

Her full, soft lips that tasted like wine and honey settled into a soft pout. Like an okay-I'll-listen-to-you expression.

"They were mostly thieves who laughed at the conventions of our world. I started selling forged paintings to tourists. I got good at it. My young face and ability with languages helped. I made money fast and the more I made, the deeper I got into their dark world."

"I thought you'd always been a boy scout." Her eyes softened.

"At first it was fun. There's a rush to pulling a good con. I liked the camaraderie of the other guys. You know brothers on the street, and all that shit. I made tons of cash, drank lots of beer, discovered sex. But the men in charge started making more and more demands of me. They wanted more."

"Like how?"

"At first, I sold small prints, then sketches and then paintings."

She nodded.

"And then..." He heard his voice crack, but he had to tell her. She had to know who he was. "They wanted me to sell myself."

"You mean..."

He shifted his gaze. Looking out the windows made talking about this stuff easier. "Tourists come to Amsterdam for many things. Some want sex."

"And you?"

"I thought I had no choice. Tante Zen had thrown me out of her house, because I never came home and she knew I was into bad stuff. I had no one but them. They had become my family."

"Women or men?"

He shrugged, but his gut wrenched. "Both, and sometimes more than one. As soon as they learned about my, uh-'stamina,' they had people paying to watch me."

"Sebastian, you don't have to tell me this."

He hadn't told anyone this much about himself before, but he kept going. "Yes I do. You think I'm some squeaky-clean knight in shining armor and I've let you think that. But beneath the armor is a guy who's taken a lot of bad turns, and who wants to build a healthy, normal life; maybe even have a family."

She closed her eyes for a moment. When she opened them again they were brimming with unspilled tears. But her voice held steady and strong. "You pulled yourself out of trouble a long time ago, before you met me. I have nothing to do with your past."

"To understand me you need to understand my past."

She nodded.

"I was seventeen and enjoying the money and the drugs. I told myself the sex was meaningless and sometimes enjoyed it. But when Alinda..." His voice became quieter.

Sadie reached over and took his hand. "Alinda?"

He looked at her. "Alinda was another sex worker two years older than me. We often worked as a team and I had feelings for her."

"What happened?"

He looked at the floor. "I found her in an alley with her throat slit. Our boss, Vlad, said a customer, a real bad ass, did it, but my gut told me it was him. He was a sick, violent asshole and had a weird thing for her. She made a point of avoiding him as much as she could. I couldn't prove he did it. It was just a feeling. I looked into his eyes and I knew. He told me to leave her body in the alley and make myself scarce."

"No police?"

"I was a prostitute addicted to heroin. Cops were my enemy."

"Heroin. So what did you do?"

"The short story: I called Xander. We'd been friends for years, but we lost touch when I took to the streets. He let me stay with him and his family adopted me. Tante Zen cheered from the sidelines."

A smile wormed its way onto his face at the memory. "I'll never forget the look on Xander's face when he saw how wasted I had become.

"He helped me pack my things at the communal house where I'd been crashing. Two thugs who acted as security for Vlad tried to stop us leaving, but Xander pulled a gun on them. A gun! I had no idea he could be such a heavy-weight."

"You kicked the heroin."

He nodded. "I had a lot of support and at the time I didn't think I deserved it. Tante Zen and the van der Valk family were there for me. I got off it just in time. I was beginning not to care if I lived or died."

"I've seen a lot of drugs in the modeling world. I'm sorry you had to go through that."

"Do they use it to stay thin?"

"That's a nice side -effect, but mostly they use it to forget their lives. They enter the world young and naïve and don't like who they become or how they're living. They get used a lot. Body and soul used."

He sighed. "I can relate to that. Did you ever...?"

"For about two months, just before I divorced Jonathon. It numbed me to the world."

"So how did you kick it?"

"The CIA found me, straightened me out and then sent me to the farm for training."

"Hmm. So that's part of your loyalty thing to them."

She nodded. The tears were gone, but her lips still held sadness. She released his hand and leaned back into the sofa. "Did Alinda have family?"

"She belonged to the streets. Her step-father sexually abused her from the time she turned six. Her mother refused to believe it. Alinda said she had no one, but when she died she was pregnant."

"She had you."

"Lot of good I was." He gripped the arms of the chair. "I should have seen it coming. I should have protected her. But the drugs stopped me from seeing anything beyond the next fix."

Sadie took a deep breath. "So that's why you're reluctant to get deeply involved with women?

You don't want to feel that responsibility and guilt again?"

"Fuck. I don't believe in psycho-babble. I just know that until I met you, I never wanted a close relationship."

"And now I'm pulling away." She bit her lower lip. "I'm sorry Sebastian."

"Sadie, you gotta give us another chance. Don't end it. Don't say anything you can't take back. It's like toothpaste pushed out of the tube, you know. Give us time."

CHAPTER 21

Cairo

*K*halid could have gone to a holy site, one of the pyramids or temples, to do his thing, but there were too many people around. The last thing he wanted was an audience. No one but him should hear what the spirits had to say to him.

He headed up to his guest room, which was larger than his whole apartment in Amsterdam. The largeness of the place blew his mind.

As he walked along the second balcony he ran into Darius, the servant who his father said would attend to his needs.

"May I get anything for you," he said in heavily accented English.

"No, thank you. But you could do one thing for me."

He bowed his head.

"Make sure no one disturbs me for the next hour."

A glint of curiosity crossed the small man's dark eyes, but he said nothing. He simply bowed again.

Once in his room, Khalid locked the door and pulled from his knapsack a candle, matches, incense and his wand. He placed a towel on the floor to act as an altar, and placed the candle and incense holder in the middle. He lit both. The incense had been prepared by his mother, in the same way it been prepared centuries ago in ancient Egypt for religious rituals. It smelled distinctly different than any he'd been able to purchase. As Khalid steadied his breathing and his mind, the sweetness of the honey and cinnamon in the kyphi filled the room.

Chanting in his mind the ancient mantra passed down to him, he continued to breathe deeply. "Open universe. Open time. Open spirit."

He lifted his wand as it began to vibrate. "I am the keeper of the Akashic Records, all of which is, and which shall be. Eternity and Everlastingness, open your portals." Energy, dark energy, flowed through his veins chilling him to the bone. His eyes stung as if slapped by a strong wind. The ritual had not been this difficult before he took his mother's life. "May I fly like a falcon. May I see the dark truth revealed."

His chest tightened. A strong presence entered his mind and he faded within myself.

"I am Ammit the soul-eater." Her voice spoke from his mouth, strong and demanding. Khalid knew her to be a female demon, described as part lion, part hippopotamus and part crocodile in the old scripts. His old self shivered within his mind, watching her take over his essence.

Khalid would have screamed if he had a voice, but he no longer had one.

He'd called on evil before, but those spirits had been undead souls that roamed the earth. Nasty, but not controlling. They had been willing to use him for their own pleasure, and his. An equal opportunity kind of gig, which he had enjoyed and respected.

Never had Khalid connected with the man-eating demon before.

"Have I already been judged?" he asked. "Doesn't that happen after I die?" The ancients believed when you proceed to the after world, the god Anubis weighed your heart and compared it to the weight of a feather. Ma'at, the goddess of justice brought the feather. If the heart was judged unworthy, Ammit, the demon now within Khalid, devoured your soul. You died a second time, to spend eternity in a state of restlessness.

The spirit world was complicated, and he didn't believe the old stories in a literal sense. He considered them warnings. But the beast within him felt a hell of a lot more powerful than a metaphor.

He tried to swallow but couldn't. He'd killed his mother and that would certainly increase the weight of his heart, soul... whatever. Maybe that's why the soul eater had come early.

But he hadn't meant to kill his mother. The spell had gone wrong and it was her fault, really. Her fault. That had to count for something. Would he be given an opportunity to speak on his own behalf?

"No," boomed Ammit, hearing the young man's thoughts. "Only the gods can judge the true heart of a man. We have no use for your words."

"I didn't mean to kill her." His voice sounded weaker than he wanted it to.

"We shall talk about that later. For now, you want guidance, and I am offering you mine." The air chilled in the room.

Guidance from a soul-eater? "At what cost?"

"What?" Her voice shook Khalid's whole body. "You dare to talk to me about cost? I am not for hire."

If I could only turn back time. "I... I..."

Her spirit slid outside his body and appeared an apparition standing before him. Ten feet tall, with the head of a crocodile, she exhaled foul air that smelled of rotting flesh. She peered down on him with beady eyes. "You want to be the most powerful sorcerer in the world. I can make it so."

With a snap of her jaws she transformed into a voluptuous, raven-haired woman his age, naked, except for the tattoos covering her honey-toned skin.

Khalid cringed. Could he work with this demon? How much more powerful would he become? "What do you want?"

A wicked smile spread across her delicate face. She didn't say anything. She didn't have to. Khalid could feel her answer in every fiber of my body. She already had what she wanted. Him.

I should have anticipated this. He had, after all, crossed a sacred boundary. His soul was doomed for eternity. Knowing this should be a source of strength for him. Should...

A tremor of regret squeezed his gut and a glimmer of hope burbled inside of him. Could he use his new power to redeem myself? Maybe save his sister? His skin prickled.

The beautiful demon raised her chin and an evil, cackling sound danced in the air between them. "There are souls so dark that redemption is impossible for them. You are a black spirit now. One of mine." She cackled some more.

"But..."

"Do not fear. If you do my bidding, I will give your eternal death some comforts. Over time you will become used to the smell of death. The screams of tortured souls will be like music. My world will become yours. It is not so bad." Her purple lips pouted.

"A sanctuary in hell?"

"You do want to live with me, don't you?" An orange glow gleamed from her eyes reminding Khalid once again that no matter how hot she looked, she was far from mortal.

"What is it you want me to do?"

"Help your father attain King Tutankhamen's scarab. Then bring it to me and we will use it for our own ends."

"But my sister..."

"Is destined to die. The scarab can give her only a few months. It cannot give her eternal life."

"What about my father? He's a violent man. Crossing him is dangerous."

"If you have the scarab, he can't touch you."

That all made sense, but she wasn't telling him what he really wanted to know. How could he phrase it?

"You idiot. Do you not realize that I hear all that is in your mind? It is not for you to question me or my purpose. But if you really want to know..."

"Yes, I do."

"I want you to use the scarab to create chaos on the mortal plane. You know the regular juicy stuff that breaks families and friends apart; jealousy between siblings, distrust and animosity between lovers, hatred for people who are different in any way. I want to weaken the world with black thoughts. Terrorize it with sin."

"And this scarab will help?"

"It is a powerful amulet crafted with great care by a holy man, endowed with the secrets of the ancient spirits. Trust me. It will make a difference. One hell of a difference." She gave a nasty chuckle.

Khalid scratched his chin. A demon who makes hell-puns? *Maybe I'm having a left-over hallucination from the party last weekend. Who knows what was in those yellow capsules. I still can't remember half of what happened for two days. Waking up spooning a complete stranger who smelled of pickled cod had sobered me quickly. Maybe what I'm experiencing now isn't real. I've never had a drug hangover like this, but...*

A lion's roar answered his meandering thoughts. "I am real." Her voice bounced off the walls and echoed through the sinews of his body. "As real as your soul. Do not underestimate me. I am a powerful demon-goddess. You may live to become the most powerful sorcerer the world has ever known, but your power will never be anything compared to mine." As she hissed, her beady eyes shone with a wickedness that sent icy waves of foreboding clawing up his back. It was all so bizarre, but all so real.

A loud banging sound caught his attention. He looked towards the door. "Master, are you all right?" Darius's voice came through the old wood.

"Yes. I told you not to disturb me."

"But all the noise in there and the smell."

Khalid looked back to the demon, but she had vanished.

"I was just... reading out loud. I like to do that."

"Get the scarab for me," Ammit's voice commanded through his trembling mind. "Do it now."

CHAPTER 22

As Chasisi stepped into Bakari's
office, he pushed the send button on his text to
Sadie. Sitting behind his desk he waved his brother
to come closer noting something about him looked
off. Even under horrendous circumstances—and
they'd had their share of those in the arms
business—Chas had kept his composure. Nothing
ruffled the man. But today he looked awful. His face
had lost color, and his dark eyes darted around the
room like a caged animal. "What's wrong?" Bakari
asked.

Chas limped over to the seat opposite his
desk and folded his lean body into it. "Khalid is like
poison. I don't want him in our home. The boy is
evil." Spittle flew through the air and his rough voice
held more malice than his words.

Anger rose in Bakari's gut like a flash flood,
but he pushed it down. "I know you are only
concerned about our family, but he is family too."

"I found him with Rashida."

Bakari glared at him. "What are you suggesting?"

Chasisi looked at the ceiling. "He has no respect for any of us. He's crude. He's base. He doesn't belong here."

Slowly releasing his breath, Bakari shook his head. "We must give him a chance. If you are concerned about Rashida, place a guard on her. I will have her mother talk to her as well. But make no mistake, Chas, I intend to make Khalid welcome in our home."

Chas stared at him for a moment then his eyes softened, as if he agreed with Bakari but it was more likely he recognized there was no purpose in continuing the argument. He took a packet of cigarillos from his chest pocket "What will you do with him when you go to London? I presume you want to be there when we take the scarab."

Bakari pushed an ash tray in his direction and nodded. "I will be leaving shortly."

Chas lit his cigarillo and inhaled deeply. Funny how the sound and smell of something so unhealthy could be comforting, but it was. Bakari enjoyed hanging out with his brother. No one understood him better. The sharp anger now completely forgotten, he looked out his window at his garden. He'd have to commend his gardening crew. It had never looked lovelier.

Bakari exhaled. Somehow he'd make everything work out. He'd do whatever he had to for his family.

After a couple of minutes, Chas spoke. "Why are you leaving so early? The heist is not planned until next week."

"I have business to attend to."

Chas's right brow rose. "What business?"

Bakari hesitated. Part of him didn't want to talk about Sadie. Chasisi would never understand his feelings for her.

Even Djeserit had counseled him to pursue her. Like an unfinished story, he needed to see how it would unfold, had to see what possibilities the future held for the two of them. Maybe she was playing him but, on the off-chance she wasn't...

"Bakari?"

He had to tell Chas. Not only was he his brother and closer to him than anyone else in the world, he was also the head of security for the family. While he didn't like to think that Sadie Stewart meant to harm him, he had to consider all possibilities. "I'm meeting with a woman. I'll take two of our best guards for protection, but I don't anticipate trouble."

"A woman?"

"I met her some time ago, and she called me, and..." He left the rest for Chas's imagination.

Blowing smoke rings in the air Chasisi leaned back. "It's hard for me to imagine a woman who would pull you away from Cairo now, when Khalid has just arrived, and when we plan a most difficult heist." He sucked on his cigarillo again and blew more smoke. "And then there's the fact that you have several women here to screw."

Bakari said nothing, hoping Chas would leave it alone.

Tapping the arm of his chair with his free hand Chas's body stilled. He leaned forward, eyes wide. "Not her."

"Who I sleep with is my business."

"Not when the CIA is involved." He waved his hands in the air. "You don't fuck the CIA."

"I have to see her."

"Let me take some precautions then." Chas growled. His face turned red. "I tell you she's dangerous. Everything about her is dangerous."

Bakari laughed. Sadie's soft, moss-green eyes—the eyes of a temptress came to mind—followed quickly by her sensuous mouth and body. He'd never wanted a woman more than he wanted her, even if it were only for one night. "Dangerous is good for the blood."

"Like hell. Two guards won't be enough."

"Then assign more. I don't care who watches over me, as long as they give me some privacy."

"I tell you this is a really stupid thing to do. I'll send Gahiji to follow her. He won't let her, or anyone else, harm you." Chasisi stood up. "Where is she now?"

"New York."

CHAPTER 23

New York

After Sebastian closed the
door quietly behind him, Sadie was left alone, utterly
alone. Was she crazy? He'd opened himself up to her,
made himself totally vulnerable and exposed, and
still she had told him to go. She shook her head as if
that would clear it. Never had she loved anyone the
way she loved Sebastian, yet she pushed him away.

Tears filled her eyes, which made her mad.
She didn't have time to cry, damn it. And CIA
operatives didn't cry. She picked up one of her
favorite books an old-fashioned spy story and threw
it against the wall. It hit with a dull thud. Then she
picked up a small glass statue from Venice and
threw it at the wall. It shattered into a million pieces.
That felt better. A bit. Who the frig needed men?
They were nothing but trouble.

Puppy had scurried under the sofa and
watched her with his big brown eyes.

Grabbing a broom from the hall closet, she grumbled. She needed to be focused, but she felt anything but. The statue had left a mark on the wall. Would that be all she'd have left to remember him by? He'd opened himself up to her. He'd loved her, as no man had ever loved her before. The way he made her feel was something she could never forget, cherished beyond words. It wasn't just that he could make her laugh, though he did, often. Or that he was terrific in bed, which he was. It was all about the magic between them.

Puppy attacked the broom and she found herself in a tug of war. She let him drag it away from her and went to the window to check on the weather. The strong wind pushed against the glass and the expected heavy rains poured down, beating so loudly she could hear it though the double-glazed windows.

The black sky and rain made everything dark. No one walked on the sidewalks and only one car motored along the usually busy street. So unlike the New York she loved.

Before turning on the TV for an update, she tore Puppy away from her broom. He'd already eaten part of it. She grabbed herself a glass of water.

Leroy Jones, her favorite anchor came onto the screen with his heavy New York accent and ice blue eyes. Getting the news from someone she'd learned to trust made her shoulders drop a little.

"Breaking news," he said in his deep resonant voice that made her backbone vibrate. "The path of hurricane Bob has veered east into the Atlantic. The city will continue to be battered by the edge of the system. We can expect storm force winds of fifty-four miles per hour—ten on the Beaufort scale—for most of the night, and torrential rain. Meteorologists say the hurricane will not, I repeat, will not, hit us directly, as previously expected. People are still cautioned to stay inside during the storm, but are no longer encouraged to evacuate. Again... Hurricane Bob will not hit us directly." He leaned his long body back in his chair and took off his glasses. That's why she liked him. Unlike other media gurus he didn't just announce the news, he felt it. "Bob will not be another Sandy. I'd like to add—" She muted him at this point, hearing the buzz of her cell-phone.

A message from Bakari. Finally! "Fly to London. I will send a car to the airport for you. We can spend a few days together. Take care."

He sure didn't waste time. Would he rush things in bed, too? At least it would be over quickly. Laughing at her own sick joke, she ran a hand through her hair. Time to pack.

Puppy scratched at her leg. The little guy had sharp nails. She picked him up and pulled him in for a cuddle. Maybe having a dog wouldn't be such a bad thing. Time to get to work.

First call, a dog sitter. But they'd only just met. Looking into the soft, playful eyes of the puppy she sighed. Damn that Mitch. He knew how to get to her. This little sweetheart had wormed his way right into her heart, despite the fact that she'd peed on her best friend's shoe and pooped on her new flooring. She stroked his soft fur. Puppy had to be the softest and cuddliest dog ever. She nuzzled him. Some tough spy.

Mitch said she could call his vet friend to take care of the dog, but she didn't want Puppy to be institutionalized at such a young age.

The ting-ting sound of a message came through. A report from Jeremiah on her new neighbor Beatrice. She scanned it quickly. The woman had bought the apartment a month ago. Real Name - Harriet Lewinski, born 1950 Hungary, moved to US in 1960, lived most of her life in Vegas, first a show girl with some talent, then a mistress to a series of mobsters. In 1995 she became the bookkeeper for Big Cajones aka Salvadore Sanchez.

Sadie smiled. Beatice was a mobster gal, an old-time moll, who got into her own business on the side. *I'm getting to like this woman. Not perfectly clean, but I'm guessing loyal and soft on the rule of the law.* That could be a good thing. At the end of the report Jeremiah wrote, "Don't see any ties to our business, yet, but I'll keep looking."

"Have you got her telephone number?"

Cole gave it to her and clicked off.

Beatrice would do. Sadie phoned her.

"Honey, you want me to do what?" said Beatrice.

"Take care of my puppy until my friend Mitch returns to town. It will be only for a day and the pup..." Of course she didn't know how long it would really be, but a couple days would be a good start.

"How'd you get my numba" Every word dripped with her vintage New York accent.

"The supe," Sadie lied. "Name your price. I'm desperate."

Beatrice cackled. She actually cackled.

Sadie's eyebrows knitted together. "I have to leave town," she said.

"I used to have a dog, a white miniature poodle I called Precious. Okay, I'll do it, but not for money."

Not for money? This is New York. Sadie waited.

"You can pay me back by being a good neighbor."

What the hell did that mean? "Okaay," Sadie said.

Beatrice hung up. Great. Now she owed a favor to a neighbor who was tight with the Mafia. How many other unwritten spy rules could she break today?

Sadie tried to pack with the puppy at her heels, but the adorable little fluff-ball kept getting in the way. She stepped on him twice and then he stole a pair of her nylons and went for a run. She caught up with him and walked him over to Beatrice's apartment with a bag full of supplies and a card with Mitchell's phone number on it.

Beatrice answered her door after the first knock, with the sound of three dead bolts being slid open. The curlers were gone from her head and her platinum blond hair had been combed into a perfect bob. Her housecoat had been replaced by a shocking pink outfit. Brighter than any pink Sadie had ever seen. Beatrice's spandex pants clung to her thin legs. Her floral-pink shirt exposed two inches of wrinkled and freckled cleavage. Around her neck she wore one large, gold cross. After giving her body a sweep, Sadie made a point of keeping her eyes on the woman's face.

Beneath a cheap pair of false eyelashes were hazel eyes, the kind that showed little emotion, like they'd seen enough in their lifetime. Sadie stepped past her into the apartment with the puppy. It had been built exactly like her own, but furnished in a kind of boho, Vegas, garage-sale style that brought a smile to Sadie's face.

"She looks a bit like a poodle," Beatrice said as she bent down and picked up Puppy.

"I think he's a Labradoodle."

Beatrice didn't say anything to that, but the look she gave could have fried a tomato. Obviously not a fan of yuppy dog breeds.

"What's his name?" Beatrice rubbed under the puppy's ears, sending his tail into a wagging frenzy.

"Puppy, until I can think of a better name."

"With his big brown eyes he's a woman killer. I'd call him Casanova."

"That's it. That's his name. A perfect fit."

They watched the puppy for a few minutes, then Sadie remembered her mission. "He's a good puppy," she said, lying again.

"You in some kinda trouble, honey?" The woman's eyes swept over Sadie.

"I need to get to London, that's all." Damn, she shouldn't have mentioned her destination. She was really losing it. Time to get her head back into the game.

"A man?"

"Something like that." Truth always worked better.

Beatrice nodded and scratched Casanova behind his right ear. The puppy nuzzled her back.

Sadie put the bag of supplies by the kitchen counter and headed for the door. She turned back to take one more look at her puppy.

"Hope he's worth it," said Beatrice.

Funny how she knew it was about a man.

CHAPTER 24

*D*ressed in black yoga pants and a loden-green jacket, Sadie boarded the first flight to London three hours later. Bakari had pulled strings to get her a seat on the overbooked flight. Sitting in first class, she sipped water and reviewed the material forwarded by Jeremiah. The information boiled down to three things: what the CIA knew about Bakari's plans, or at least said they knew; what they wanted her to do; and a backup strategy.

What they knew: Bakari planned to steal the scarab to save his daughter. The amulet would be shown to the public at Highclere castle for the first time on Wednesday. A ticket under her own name would be held for her at the door.

Wednesday. That gave her three days to find out more. Seventy-two hours. A team of Bakari's men flew into London yesterday. Their location and plans were unknown.

Would Gahiji, Bakari's torture loving sidekick be one of them? She shuddered and read on. Bakari boarded a plane an hour ago, also heading for London.

Bakari's wacko plan to steal another amulet had started. How could he still believe that pretty objects from the past could heal his daughter? He seemed like such an intelligent man. Someone had filled his mind with powerful superstitions. Could she change his thinking? His beliefs? That wouldn't be easy. He had constructed his own warped religion.

But if she could change his mind... The scarab would be safe. So would a lot of lives, that were about to be put at risk.

George, a CIA operative she'd worked with many times over the years, would be her back-up. He'd flown into London from Belgium and would tail her from the airport. More backup would be called in as needed. Her MI 5 liaison would be Jasper Willington, an old friend with a reputation for fast thinking in the field. They had history, mostly good. As long as he stayed out of her way and played his part, things would work out.

What exactly did they expect her to do? She re-read Jeremiah's report hoping to find more details. Towards the end, Jeremiah wrote: "Kia believes Rashida's illness has pushed Bakari's mind over the brink of sanity. To quote her: 'He's always been highly volatile. He's even more dangerous and unpredictable now.'" Great news

Jeremiah finished with: "That is why we are sending you in. Bakari's men have prepared another shipment of arms for the Islamic State. If we stop him now, we can save lives."

Kia was a top CIA profiler and she was rarely wrong. Could the news get any worse? Sadie exhaled slowly. Bakari was losing his marbles and in league with barbarians. What the hell was Jeremiah suggesting? Take him out any way, at any cost? She wasn't a hit woman. Far from it.

She ran a hand through her hair. She didn't have Kia's fancy psych degrees, but she knew men. Bakari had not shown himself to her as the power-hungry lunatic she'd expected. Yeah, she'd read the CIA dossier on him. He'd been an international bad-ass since his late teens, selling weapons to anyone with money, but that wasn't the whole story.

She drank more water. Her, "must hydrate on flights," mantra interrupted her thoughts. She'd need to be in peak condition when she arrived.

Closing the message screen on her cell-phone she plugged in her ear phones and turned on some light rock music to soothe her nerves. History was a collection of opinions, at best. It didn't really matter what had been written in the CIA reports. Sadie knew the man, knew he wasn't proud of everything he'd done, but that he'd done it for his family. He had integrity and good intentions. Well... some.

The image of his beheaded wife, Safa, came to mind. How much of the violence attributed to him had been Dead Eyes' fault? That was her name for Gahiji, one of Bakari's henchmen, a man so dark and evil it made her flesh crawl to be near him.

"Bakari gives the orders," cautioned her inner voice. "Bakari is in control."

Damn that voice.

And what about his brother, Chasisi? He'd been at the Met Museum when the last heist went down. Sources said he acted as Bakari's right-hand man. How many orders did he give?

Still, her gut told her that Bakari was in charge, always in charge. She'd met few men as alpha as him.

Could she turn him? Or would she have to trap him? Kill him? She rubbed the bridge of her nose. One way or another she'd get her man.

The miles ticked slowly by. She'd seduce him. There'd be no putting him off with innuendo this time. When it came to pillow talk, she'd manipulate him as best she could. It wasn't the greatest plan, but it was a start.

Her throat dried, and her stomach felt heavy. She'd flirted a lot as a spy, but this time she had to be ready to do more. Jeremiah had warned her that it would change her. He'd cautioned her against it. But a spy has to do whatever it takes in the field to meet their objective and stay alive.

It was just sex. And it wasn't as though she hadn't slept with her share of men. She'd fake the passion. The old—"shut your eyes and do it for the flag."

Could she act totally turned-on with a man who sold guns to terrorists? To a man almost twenty years older than herself? A man who had three living wives and one he buried in the sand? A man who intrigued her with his charm, but didn't flip her switch physically? And, worst of all—to a man who wasn't Sebastian?

Sebastian would be furious, but she pushed her thoughts and feelings for him away. She had a job to do, and no one in the world could do it better.

The plane landed and she disembarked. With her head held high, she strode through customs to look for her driver. She hoped he'd send Eboni and scanned the crowds for her face. Her hope died when she saw *him*. Standing to the side, with a scowl so dark it would make the devil flinch, stood Dead Eyes. When he saw her, he spat on the ground.

CHAPTER 25

Groaning, Sadie walked up to Dead Eyes. Without any change in his scowl he grunted, turned and walked towards the exit. His communication style had not improved since they last met. Nor had his body odor. Sadie followed rolling her carry-on bag behind her. He hailed a cab and she sat in the back next to him, but as far from him as possible. His pungent body odor filled the space—part garlic and part him.

Sadie looked out the window. Dense traffic sped away from Heathrow in the low light of the autumn afternoon. A low ceiling of clouds held the city captive in a blanket of subdued colors. Thirteen million people live in London, one of the largest global cities on the planet, known for its financial district and cultural sites. But despite that, London for her was a "gray."

She often thought in colors and London was a definite gray, a place where nature had been pushed to the edges and replaced with a dull cityscape of concrete, filled with grim people who wore gray and black every day of their lives. It didn't have the *joie de vivre* of Paris, a passionate pink to her mind, the hip vibe of Amsterdam, an orange, or the electric buzz of New York, a neon yellow. It suited business men and academics, but not her.

She looked over at Dead Eyes, but he didn't respond. His eyes, darker than the night, stared forward as if the leather back of the driver's headrest had a message from Allah inscribed in it.

Shifting her gaze back to the street, her mind ticked through her present list of concerns. She could ask the stinky gorilla some questions, like where the hell was he taking her, but he wouldn't answer. He mostly grunted, and their last conversation had ended with him putting her in a choke hold and throwing her against a wall. The visceral memory of him squeezing her neck made her rub it. She'd thought he was going to kill her.

Forty-five minutes later the taxi stopped. She'd expected a fancy hotel, but instead found herself walking up the steps of a charming Italian Villa, painted white, surrounded by an ornate concrete wall. It had three floors. A pair of bay windows on the first two floors and balconies on the third gave it an early twentieth century look. The door opened when she arrived at the steps.

A maid dressed in a proper black uniform with white ruffled lace at the buttoned up neckline and the end of long sleeves greeted her. She had a dour face, unusually long and lean that held little expression. No light reflected in her small, gray, eyes, and Sadie wondered if they'd ever known curiosity, let alone joy. A strong smell of soap emanated from her body. Sadie shuddered. It was as if the woman had stepped from the pages of a Dickens novel and would soon be scurrying back to tend to a gang of delinquent orphans.

"Welcome to Mr. Al-Sharif's residence. You are expected." She held the door open wide and waved for Sadie to enter. "My name is Elizabeth. I will do everything I can to make your stay comfortable."

Comfortable? A polite smoke and mirrors comment. Although the maid had a tidy uniform and refined British accent, her intent to *manage* Sadie reminded her of her visit to Bakari's home in Cairo. She would never feel comfortable in the home of an arms-dealer. "Does Bakari own this house?" she asked.

"Yes," the woman said as Sadie strode past her into the foyer. "It's his home when he comes to London. Sometimes other members of his family stay here as well. The manor has five bedroom suites and a large entertainment area suitable for holding small parties."

Interesting. Why hadn't the home, and its blueprints, been added to the Anubis file? Wonder how many things never made it on paper, when it came to Bakari. He'd been involved with the CIA for years, and she'd learned the hard way that what her bosses knew about him and what they told her were two different things. Had his thirst for power spread tentacles into the agency itself? Nothing like working for people who are in bed with arms dealers.

Sadie scanned the entrance, which itself was the size of her own New York living room area. Its twelve-foot ceiling gave it an expansive feel. A thick Arabian rug with a red and black design covered most of the polished wooden floor. To her right, she could see through a large open doorway into a grand dining room large enough to seat twenty. An identical doorway on her left opened into what looked like a study or meeting room. Three chairs surrounded a large glass- topped desk that didn't have anything on it. Directly in front of her, behind a round mahogany accent table was a grand Scarlett O'Hara stairway. To one side of it was a hallway. To the other a small, open door.

Sadie stepped towards the door, because it was an anomaly in this entrance where everything had been finished on a grand scale, and glimpsed a gourmet kitchen filled with shiny stainless-steel appliances, large enough to cater a small army.

The white walls of the foyer, pristine and smooth, gave the place a clean look, but made Sadie grimace. No amount of white paint could white-wash Bakari's evil deeds. What secrets lay behind these thick, Edwardian walls?

Sadie turned and made direct eye-contact with the maid. "Elizabeth, how nice to meet you. Please show me to my room."

"Yes, madam. Follow me. I'll have Rupert bring up your bag."

Rupert? That did it. Could this place be any more British? The scent of the long stem roses, sitting in a vase on the lobby table, followed her up the stairs. The maid took each step with care, as though she had a medical condition that impeded her movement. That made it less likely that she would be one of Bakari's soldiers in disguise. The woman was too old to be one of his lovers. So what exactly was she? A proper maid to keep up appearances? Maybe, but unlikely. Bakari's people all had their roles in his business.

Stopping half-way up, Sadie turned around to look for Dead Eyes, but he'd vanished into the woodwork. He was damn good at that. The only thing he was better at was jumping out of it. When they neared the second-floor landing, she asked, "Is Mr. Al-Sharif home?"

"No. He sends his regrets for not meeting you himself. He will be in sometime soon. A dinner has been planned for the two of you at seven."

"Seven?" It was already eight o'clock.

"Tomorrow evening. If you are hungry I can bring you a meal from our kitchen. I know the cook has roast beef and squid in her fridge."

Squid? Seriously? "That's all right. I ate on the plane." And she had protein bars packed. On the second floor was a hallway with four doors. Sadie followed her to the first on the right. The maid held the door open and held it for her.

Stepping into the guest room, was like jumping down the rabbit hole. While the house so far had seemed traditionally restored Edwardian, this room looked as if it had come straight from the tales of the Arabian Nights. It looked to be twelve feet by fourteen. The ceiling was lower on this floor, maybe ten feet. Carnal red drapes hung along the side walls. On the wall opposite her a large bay window looked over the street. An exquisite, plush

Arabic rug in red tones covered the floor. No sign of white here.

An unusually tall, king size bed encased with a red curtain, dominated the room, like an altar. The curtain had been pulled back, revealing pillows in rich prints covering the top half of a red bedspread. Silk. On the bedside table a vase of flowers had been set and a card leaned on it.

Against the wall to her right, a First World War-era wooden vanity rested. Against the left wall stood a writing desk, same vintage. The room had an old world, sexy feel to it, which she might have enjoyed if she was planning to meet a man other than Bakari.

She turned to ask Elizabeth for a cup of tea, but the woman had vanished. A man appeared. He had to be Rupert, a rather emaciated, middle-aged gentleman in a uniform, with a well-cared for mustache. He placed her bag at the entrance of the room, nodded to her and left.

After locking the door she hatched her plan. First, she'd sweep the room for bugs. She wouldn't bother trying to be discreet about it. Bakari knew her background, and it was reasonable that she should be concerned about her privacy. Then she'd update Jeremiah. That done, she'd ask for tea in the dining room to get a better sense of the layout of the house and the number and purpose of the people in it. Later that night, when the lights went out and the servants went home, or at least to bed, she'd have a good look at the house.

A nice, warm feeling filled her at the thought of uncovering Bakari's secrets. She was closer now and the thrill of the chase coursed through her blood.

Jeremiah had sent a new bug detector to her at the airport before she left New York. This one looked like a thumb drive. It flashed red when it detected listening devices and blue when it found cameras. Going over every inch of the space took thirty minutes. Two cameras focused on the bed, one listening device was on a land-line telephone with another underneath the desk. The bathroom appeared to be clean. She collected all the bugs and put them in the clear vase that held roses. The plopping sound as they hit the water gave her a warm rush. *Oh yeah, it felt good to be a spook.*

Not wanting to risk a phone call, she sent a text to Jeremiah on her company phone, which she had strapped to the inside of her thigh. It used the latest encryption software. "Arrived safely. Alone for the night. Will contact." She pushed send. Checking her other mobile, she found she had three messages from Mitchell and one from Sebastian. They'd have to wait.

Pulling on the long, servant cord that hung beside the bed, she expected to hear a sound, but didn't. She pulled it again. Two minutes later, she heard a discreet knock on her door.

"Come in," Sadie called out.

Elizabeth opened the door and gave her the same weak smile she'd worn downstairs.

"I'd like tea," Sadie said with an arrogant attitude.

"I can bring you a tray, if you'd like," said the woman as if it were no trouble at all for her to run up and down the stairs.

"I'd rather sit in the dining room, if that's possible. I feel..." Sadie swept her arm around the room. "Claustrophobic here. To be honest I was hoping to meet the rest of the household as well." She kept her tone haughty, like an aristocratic, bitch wannabe. The woman would really have no choice but to accept her request, whether she wanted to or not. Still, Sadie held her breath for a moment in anticipation.

"Yes madam. As you wish. I'll get the cook to put the kettle on." She turned and walked out stiffly. An act? Arthritis?

Sadie took a minute to freshen her lipstick and pull a brush through her hair. Inside her sleeve she slid a tiny camera, just in case something interesting turned up. Show time.

CHAPTER 26

On the way down to tea, Sadie reaffirmed that there were four doors on her floor, probably four bedrooms. The next floor would have the fifth. And what else? She'd figure that out later. Downstairs was for eating, entertainment and business. The layout was practical, which suited Bakari the business man.

From the bottom of the stairs she looked towards his office, but she couldn't see anything. The enormous wooden door had been closed. She turned towards the dining room.

A proper English tea had been set up on the enormous dining-room table. On one end, a fine china plate, tea cup and saucer had been set on a white-linen tablecloth. In front of that a three-tiered china serving dish laden with small sandwiches, scones and sweets. The scene belonged in a foodie magazine.

When she sat down, Elizabeth appeared. Sadie's chest tightened. How did she appear so damn quickly, when she walked so slowly? Sadie hadn't heard one footstep. Maybe the woman was part spy.

The maid perched at her side. "Sugar or milk, madam?"

"Let me pour." She never liked the tradition of the English *mother* preparing her tea. Of course the intention was to indulge you, but it made her feel smothered and useless.

The woman arched one heavily drawn black brow.

"Elizabeth, I'd like to be alone. I'm American. I can take care of myself." Again she used a haughty tone that the servant would not, could not, ignore.

The maid nodded and vanished. Damn that woman was quick. This time Sadie caught her exit a small door to the left that didn't even look like a door. It looked more like a secret passage. Interesting.

Sadie poured her tea, added a dash of milk and took a sip. Heavenly. A loose, black tea steeped perfectly. The malty flavor suggested Assam; the golden coppery taste, Kenya, a fruity touch, South India. She took another sip. Hmm. There was a piquant edge to it. Ceylon? Definitely Chinese for the oaky note. A lovely blend. The aroma alone revitalized her energy.

On the bottom tier of the serving tray, were tiny sandwiches made with white bread cut into squares and triangles: cucumber and butter, smoked salmon and cream cheese, and egg salad. On the second tier a layer of scones said, "Eat me," to her calorie deprived body. A small bowl of Devonshire cream sat among them and on the table several small crystal jars of jam: raspberry, blackberry and strawberry.

Lots of food. Would anyone in the house try to poison her?

On the top plate were tiny petit-fours. She sighed at the one topped with a sliced strawberry covered in dark chocolate. Two things she truly loved were chocolate and strawberries. It looked worthy of its calories.

Sadie looked around. The wall facing the street opened onto a small stone terrace. The French doors were slightly ajar, letting in a cool autumn breeze. It stirred the sheer curtains. On each side of the French doors large paintings had been hung. To the left was a scene of wildflowers in the countryside. Impressionist in style, it looked like a Monet with dabs of delicate colors. The other painting was of a vase of flowers and looked like a take-off of Van Gogh's *Sunflowers,* with sharp bold colors. Bakari may be the meanest son of a bitch on the planet, but he sure liked flowers.

On the inside wall was an open doorway that led to a hall, and the hidden doorway through which Elizabeth had disappeared. The smell of cinnamon baking wafted in the air.

On the other wall was a portrait of Bakari. His eyes, darker than the night dominated his face. His black hair had started graying at the temples when the portrait had been done, so it was probably fairly new. The mole on his left cheek had been made fainter than in real life and his shoulders broader than she remembered, but otherwise the artist had captured the man. He looked regal and powerful; yet at the same time a sadness lingered at the corners of his mouth. Interesting company for high tea. She took another sip.

Two closed circuit TV cameras, mounted in the corners of the ceiling focused on her. There'd been no attempt to hide them. She took another sip of tea and enjoyed its warmth spreading down her throat. Her shoulders ached from the long flight.

In enemy territory one had to anticipate problems, but the odds of someone ambushing her at tea seemed remote. She took a deep breath and told herself to relax. For one thing Bakari's people must know that he wanted her to be treated well, that he had amorous plans for her. For another, it would be too obvious to attack her here, and the culprit would probably lose his head.

The food looked so good, she had to indulge. She popped the strawberry topped petite-four into her mouth, letting the flavors of fresh fruit, and chocolate mix on her palate, feeling the texture of the thin, crisp wafer inside.

Maybe being Bakari's mistress wouldn't be all that bad. She'd just have to learn to stomach his heinous crimes. She poured more tea in her cup.

She eyed a cucumber sandwich next. How many calories could a vegetable have? Her professional model mind went into calculation. One teaspoon of butter thirty-five calories; two small pieces of bread twenty; the hidden teaspoon of mayonnaise thirty-five; and the cucumber, a big fat zero. Total ninety calories for two bites of yumminess. What the hell. She picked it up. She shouldn't, but you only live once.

A loud gong startled her as she munched. She checked her watch: nine o'clock. The sound could have stirred the dead. She expected Elizabeth to rush to the door, but a minute later Dead Eyes appeared. A plain, white, long-sleeved, cotton shirt rolled up to his elbows hung loose over black cargo pants. His black, leather shoulder holster was in place. He'd also have a knife strapped to his ankle. He looked at a video screen mounted beside the door and grunted. A second man appeared with a Glock pointed at the door. He moved to stand to the left.

The gong sounded again, and before its echo finished the door had been opened to reveal a tiny young woman dressed in an Express Mail uniform holding two packages: a cardboard cylinder and a small box wrapped in brown paper. The box was about eight by eleven on top, and two inches deep. It looked like it could contain a bundle of photocopy paper.

The woman appeared to be about twenty. Her long blond hair had been pulled up into a ponytail and stuffed into the company blue and white, ball hat with its Speedy Guy logo on the front. Her face looked gaunt, like she ate too many cucumbers and when she looked at Dead-Eyes she winced and took a step back. Smart woman.

He didn't say anything at all. The force of his stare threatened well enough. The young woman handed him a device to sign, which he did, and then she gave him the packages.

Sadie swallowed her sandwich and took another sip of tea. She took a compact out of her purse and applied lipstick, so she could watch the action at the door through the tiny mirror without being obvious.

After the door closed with a solid thunk, the soldier-guy took the packages and followed Dead Eyes to the office door. Dead Eyes looked around, then used a key to gain entry. The two disappeared inside. An old fashioned key lock. She could handle that.

The scones begged to be eaten, so she indulged in one, adding blackberry jam. She drank another cup of tea.

Tonight, when the house settled, she'd have a good look at Bakari's office. The thought warmed her more than the tea.

CHAPTER 27

As Sadie put down her napkin, the gong rang again, only this time it sounded softer. Clearly someone monitored the front door and called the appropriate person when needed. This time Elizabeth appeared. Not a hair out of place. Sadie poured herself the dregs from the tea pot and opened her compact.

She had never met the man who strode in, but she'd read about him in Bakari's dossier. Khalid Badru, an Amsterdamer, rumored to be the illegitimate son of Bakari. He'd recently been taken in by the family. His young wiry body moved with an unsettled energy as if he wasn't sure he wanted to be there. He talked in quiet tones with the maid, then stopped mid-sentence, turned and stared at Sadie. He'd made her.

***

Khalid turned towards the source of the eyes he felt on his skin. A woman seated in the dining room watched him through her make-up mirror. He brushed past the maid and strode towards her.

"Good afternoon," he said.

The woman closed her mirror case before he made it to her side. She looked up at him with cat-like, moss-green eyes that beckoned. He took a second breath.

"Good afternoon," she replied. American accent.

"My name is Khalid Badru. This is my father's home."

"It's a pleasure to meet you. My name is Sadie Stewart. I'm a..." she paused to sound demure, "friend of Bakari's."

Ah, the American whore. "It's a pleasure to meet you. My father speaks of you with the warmest of words." *And he can't wait to fuck you.*

As she nodded her long mane of red hair moved and the light caught and held on the wavy tendrils that fell to her breasts. Khalid could see why his father would take risks for her. He shouldn't stare, but it was hard not to.

Her full, sensual lips begged to be kissed. His eyes scanned downward, down her long neck to her firm breasts and trim waist. It would be heaven to have his hands on this woman. He swallowed and hoped his face hadn't turned pink.

"I was just having tea. If you'd like to join me..." Her elegant hand waved to another chair and following its sweeping motion he noticed the fancy tray of food on the table.

But his words wouldn't come. Pure, raw sensuality flowed from her, filling the room with an erotic magnetism, choking him. He tried to read her, but his blood rushed to his groin. He sat down barely feeling the chair beneath him.

"Khalid is an interesting name. What does it mean?" Even her voice had a throaty quality that made him think of sex. Hot sex. Hot sex with her.

"Immortal. It means, well immortal." Could he sound any more lame?

The brittle-looking maid came in and lifted the teapot. "I'll bring a fresh pot," she said and left through a side door.

The beating sound of a low flying helicopter took his attention for a second. Must be a medical emergency nearby.

Sadie brought him back to the room with a wicked laugh, the kind you usually hear in a bedroom. "Have you the balls to live up to your name?"

Balls? Did she just say balls? *Love bawdy women.* "And then some."

She pouted her lips and leaned his way. Khalid could smell the fruity shampoo in her thick mane of auburn hair, the delicate fragrance of her expensive perfume and beneath all that her musky womanness. "I don't doubt that," she said.

Suddenly Khalid felt like he could leap tall buildings. And he'd do it, if he could get between her legs.

Don't be stupid. She's playing you. He gritted his teeth, but that didn't really help. Sweat trickled down the back of his neck. He looked into her fathomless green eyes and tried once again to read her.

She reached out for his hand and tapped it, making it once again impossible for him to think with his head. His heart raced.

He pulled his hand back, feeling his cheeks burn. *Get a fucking hold of yourself.* His bodily reactions to being so close to her were embarrassing. He forced himself to lean back.

"Is something wrong?" she cooed. In her sexy voice was an awareness of her own sexual power over him, and that only turned him on more.

The woman had a hex on him. Could she be a sorceress? He extended his senses as best as he could with his hard-on clouding his thoughts. After a minute, his shoulders relaxed. No, she wasn't one of them. She was simply all woman, sensual and sexual and...

"Good afternoon." Bakari's dominant voice came from the doorway.

CHAPTER 28

*B*akari had taken a helicopter from the airport. Usually Gahiji would pick him up in a car, but today he wanted to get to the house as soon as he could. Sadie Stewart would be waiting for him. Between reading business reports and worrying about Rashida, he'd had time to think about his evening with her. Would she be as eager to be with him as she sounded on the phone?

He entered through the back door, dismissed his two body guards and headed towards the dining room where he could hear voices. Hers soft and enticing, just like he remembered. His? It couldn't be.

He made it to the doorway. Indeed, his son Khalid sat with her. His staff had informed him that he'd arrived in London, but he didn't expect to find him with her.

"Good evening," Bakari said. They both looked up. A wide smile spread across her face making her look lovelier than he remembered. She had to be the most beautiful woman he'd ever laid eyes on. His son, all red-faced, looked like he'd choked on the pit of a date. No doubt the charms of the American had worked their magic on him.

Bakari's heart beat faster. He'd have to accept that other men would be attracted to her. She was a woman all men would want. And maybe it wasn't a bad thing that the two of them had met. He could ask Khalid what he thought of her later. Get a read on her. He didn't want to believe Chasisi's warnings that the woman was playing him.

He wanted Sadie so badly it hurt. If he approached her slowly he may be able to have her all to himself. That would be something. Holding her eyes with his, he walked up to her and lifted her right hand to his lips. Her fingers were long and delicate and felt softer than silk. Her scent hit him like a tidal wave, so distinct it made him as hard as a lamp-post.

When he kissed her on the cheek, a trembling sensation started at the base of his spine and rose. He'd never wanted a woman more. Self-restraint would be nearly impossible. "You look so beautiful, Sadie."

Her full lips pulled into a warm smile, telegraphing it was meant only for him. He swallowed, trying to regain some composure and turned towards his son. "I thought you'd planned to stay in Cairo."

Khalid gave him a stubborn teenage face, his eyes sullen, his lips curving. "I thought I'd be more useful to you here."

"Perhaps." Bakari stared at him hard. "We could have talked about it."

The younger man shrugged.

An uncomfortable silence filled the room as the two men stared at one another.

Sadie broke the stand-off. "I think I'll head for bed. Flights tire me out." She put her hand gently around Bakari's arm and gave it a gentle squeeze.

"I have planned a dinner for us tomorrow. Seven o'clock?"

"Just the two of us?" she cooed.

"Definitely."

CHAPTER 29

After locking her bedroom door, Sadie climbed onto her enormous bed and took out her company cell-phone. She sent a text to Jeremiah. "Bakari and Khalid Badru are here. Papers and a parcel arrived and were put in the office. I'll look around. I have a dinner date tomorrow night." She clicked off.

On her personal phone she had messages: two from Mitch, and one from Knickers, a lady she loathed, who wanted her to do a magazine shoot next month. Sadie would need to answer the texts later. She lay back on the bed and looked up at the wooden canopy.

Khalid gave her the creep-chills. There was something odd, very odd, about that one. Bakari was just as she remembered him, a lion of a man with a bad-ass temperament. She'd see how far she could bend him.

In the meantime, it would be good to know more about the schematics of the house and what was in the cylinder and box stashed in the locked office. She stretched her legs and wiggled her toes. She would start her search at the top of the house and work down. It would be easier to do later that at night, when there was less likelihood of running into anyone.

The clock on the bedside table attached to a radio read 12:30. In order to hide easily in the shadows she put on a black top to match her black yoga pants. If anyone did manage to catch up with her she would make up an alibi about exercising.

She turned on the radio and tuned it to a classical station. Then she put some pillows inside the sheets of the bed and molded them to look like a body. After giving her ruse one more examination, she put on a pair of thin, black gloves, pulled her hair up into a knot and stuffed it into a black toque.

After three deep breathes and a knock on the head for good luck she headed for the door. Hearing no movement in the hallway, she silently exited the room and closed the door behind her.

She considered looking inside the rooms on her floor, but decided to head to the stairway instead. She climbed the stairs, listening for people. No sounds. When she made it to the next landing she expected to find a hallway lined with doorways like on her floor, but instead found herself in a small foyer with only one door, painted white like the walls. It must be Bakari's penthouse suite. She listened for any sound of activity. Nothing. Leaning into the door, she put her ear against it and listened. Still, no sounds. She sniffed the air. No smells.

Reaching for the vintage crystal-glass doorknob she extended all her senses to catch any sense of people. Nothing. She tried to turn the knob, but it wouldn't budge. Locked.

She knelt down to examine the knob closer. Unlike the door to the office below, this one did not have an old fashioned key lock. It had a card scanner beneath it. Gaining access to this room would be more difficult. How many cameras were watching her right now?

If someone caught her, she'd let her hair tumble and she'd claim to be exercising and perhaps a little curious. Would Dead Eyes believe that? Not likely. He was one of only three men in her life who were immune to her charms. Damn him and his evil eyes. She stole back down the stairs.

Descending to the first floor, she listened for movement. The busy noises of day-time activities had stopped, but she could hear some clinking in the kitchen. Maybe someone was having a late night snack.

She tiptoed into the dining room and went to the smaller door Elizabeth through which disappeared into. The knob turned and she opened the door onto a narrow hallway. She entered and closed the door quietly behind her, and flicked on her small flashlight.

To her right, four yards down the hall was a door. Probably the kitchen. The sound of voices came from there.

Holding her breath, she tiptoed past them. The corridor ended in another seven yards at a closed door. To its right rose an old, spiral metal staircase, like those found in many old houses.

She had to be directly behind the grand, Scarlett O'Hara stairway.

The spiral stairway went straight down. Down? They were at the street level. There must be a basement. Great. Dead Eyes had his own dungeon to play in. She bit her bottom lip.

If her sense of direction was right, the door could lead to Bakari's office. That would tell her more than the basement. She put her ear to the door and listened.

Hearing nothing, she tried the doorknob. It turned. Carefully she pushed open the door a sliver and peaked inside. This room would definitely have high security in it. She'd need to figure out where the control room was and take out the cameras, if she really wanted to search this room and live.

She could run into the office, grab the items the messenger had brought and run out onto the street, but that would end her chances of turning Bakari and the information might not be that useful. Better to get a look at it then leave everything in place. But, she needed to temporarily disarm the cameras. And Dead Eyes? If only she could disarm him.

She closed the door and headed back to the hidden stairway. As she stepped on the first rung it squeaked. Iron grinding on iron. She continued down, wincing every time the metal made a noise. No sign of cameras. As she descended the dank smell of earth, mold and decay assaulted her senses. Was she descending into Dante's hell? God only knew what a power crazed arms dealer who thought nothing of beheading his wife would stow in his

Edwardian London cellar. She hit dirt after the last step—black, dry and dusty dirt.

Scanning the small space with her flashlight she found two doors, one to the left and one straight ahead. Maybe the room to the left was an old bomb shelter. And the one ahead? It should lead to the street. The bomb shelter would probably be more interesting.

Its wooden handle wouldn't budge. The door had an old fashioned key lock, so after putting her ear to the door and not hearing any sound, she pulled her lock-picking jackknife from her pocket. Extending her long hook, she said a silent prayer. She readied a second pick. Her record for opening a lock like this was three minutes. Did she have the time? She slid in the hook and wiggled it around. Just as it reached a tumbler, she heard the sound of a door closing above her.

She pulled out the pick and jammed it back into her pocket. Footsteps headed towards the metal stairs. The hair on the nape of her neck rose.

The smell of garlic hit her nose. Was it her imagination? A stream of light from above shone down. She squeezed against the wall so it couldn't find her.

Beads of perspiration formed on her brow. She ran over to the other door as quietly as possible. This one had to be an escape route. No lock. She went through it and closed the door silently behind her.

It was more a tunnel than a hallway. A narrowing tunnel. Breathing became difficult, partly because her lungs resisted the cold damp air of the night and partly because adrenalin pumped through her body. Her calves tightened. A cold sweat poured down her back drenching her clothes. Her senses sharpened until she could hear the sound of rats scurrying along the pathway. She ran full speed the rest of the way, not stopping until she found herself at a circular, exit covered by a grate. She gulped in the fresh air and tried to move the cover. It didn't budge when she pushed on it the first time, or the second. Taking a step back, she kicked hard at its center. And she was free.

For about five seconds.

Barking. Lots of dogs barking.

Dogs were coming her way. It sounded like an army of hungry Doberman pinschers, rotties and pit bulls coming to get her. Couldn't she catch a break? The sound of someone shuffling along the tunnel behind her answered that question. Nope, no breaks today.

Standing on well-manicured grass she swept the area with her flashlight. She'd ended up in a small part of the back garden, set apart from the rest by a six-foot row of privet. A rose-covered arbor linked it to the main garden to her right. Beyond that stood the house.

The road had to be directly in front of her, but all she could see was the thick hedge of small, green leaves. The area wasn't lit, but the back garden was, so it wouldn't be wise to go that way. She ran over to the hedge and poked her flashlight into it.

Barking rang in her ears. The dogs were closing in on her. The hedge had to be four feet thick, and on the other side was a metal fence.

That didn't make sense. If someone had gone to the trouble of making an escape route, it should lead right to the road. Shouldn't it? She poked her arm in again about a foot. The dogs were getting louder. Her chest constricted. There had to be a way out.

Was that the smell of garlic? Had to be in her head. Shit. She pushed her hand in again. And that's when she saw the hidden doorway. It was made of fake privet. In three stuttered heart beats, she pulled on the fake branches, opened the gate and closed it behind her. Releasing a long breath she could hear the canines on the other side of the hedge jumping at the branches. A few seconds later and she'd have been dog food.

An ornate street lamp revealed a quiet road. No pedestrians. No cars. A sliver of the moon peaked from behind the clouds, giving a somber melancholy glow. Sadie started running and didn't stop until she could no longer hear the baying of the hounds, or see Bakari's house.

Every cell in her body trembled. Putting her hands on her thighs, she leaned over and concentrated on slowing her breathing. It would take a few minutes for the effects of the adrenalin to settle down. Enough time to figure out how she'd slip back into the house.

When her nerves settled she stood up, only to find herself eye to eye with Chasisi al-Sharif. On either side of him stood Doberman pinchers. A chill ran down her spine.

Dressed in a black, wool sweater, black khakis and black runners the man wore an expression of disgust. Talk about a messenger from the gates of hell.

"Good evening," Sadie said, carefully loosening her bun, so that her hair fell down over her shoulders. That was usually all she had to do to capture a man.

Silence.

His eyes stayed on hers, showing no evidence of attraction. She lifted her breasts and put her mouth into a pout. "I was running."

"From what?" His thin lips turned down into a menacing scowl and he put his hands on his hips. He didn't have Bakari's charisma, but he had an ability to instill terror in others.

"Americans don't need to run from anything. We simply run for the joy of it. It's an endorphin-addiction thing. I couldn't sleep, jet-lag and all, so I decided to run." She made her voice light, like a lame dame.

Still grimacing, he let his eyes wander over her body. His breath caught for second as he traced her hips then he cleared his throat. "Let me introduce myself. I am Chasisi al-Sharif, Bakari's brother and head of security for the family."

She was about to say something polite, but he put up his hand.

"I don't trust you."

Sadie gave him a bawdy laugh.

His eyes widened.

"Darlin', I don't trust you either," she said.

CHAPTER 30

Sadie, escorted by Chasisi and his dogs, returned to Bakari's house. Three things were clear: One, Chasisi didn't like her relationship with his brother; two, Chasisi had been told not to hurt her and; three, Chasisi would like to screw her. Talk about family drama! She could work with that. After five minutes of trying to engage him in conversation, she gave up and they walked in an unsettling silence.

After a restless night, Sadie slept late. She had a light breakfast in the dining room and then wandered around the first floor. There really wasn't much to see. The office door remained locked and the kitchen busy. She didn't dare go into the secret passage again. Not in broad daylight.

Returning to the second floor she found all but one of the four doors unlocked. Each was a replica of the suite she stayed in. Khalid must be in the fourth. She wondered what he was doing behind the locked door. Whatever it was, it made no sound.

Maybe he had gone out for the day. Sadie returned to her room.

The day passed slowly. She ignored messages from the outside world and focused on her plans for the evening. At six she began getting ready for Bakari.

Her ensuite had a soaker tub and an assortment of expensive bath products. She looked over the pretty bottles, smelling each one, not wanting to use anything that would interfere with her perfume, and settled on bubble bath solution that had little fragrance. As the water and bubbles grew she anticipated a few wonderful minutes of relaxation. There was a discreet knock on her door. Why did everyone want to visit her in the bathroom?

"Come in," she said.

Elizabeth entered the room with her prune face in place. So deep were the lines around her mouth it looked as though her grimace had been etched into her face at birth. "Madam, would you like a glass of wine, or perhaps sherry?"

How civil. Had they reinstalled cameras already? Sheesh, they were busier spying than she was. "I'd like a tall glass of ice-water," Sadie said.

Elizabeth retreated. When she returned with the requested refreshment, Sadie had submerged her long body beneath the bubbles. "Thank you."

The woman disappeared again.

After her bath, Sadie slipped on a green silk dress that hugged her curves. She brushed her hair and pulled it up into a loose chignon on top of her head. Then she put on her face. Black liner around her eyes and shades of green and silver eye-shadow gave her a sultry, in-the-mood look. Red, red lipstick with a gloss applied on top made her full lips stand out.

Then she put on her night perfume. Mitch called it her "fuck-me" elixir.

During the day Sadie wore a classic scent, Guerlain's Shalimar, created in the 1920s. Its sexy signature had a vanilla-amber base and a touch of civet and lemon that always drew attention.

But for evenings she chose a rare fragrance that rocked a room in seconds, Serge Luten's Sarrasins, a Moroccan-inflected, jasmine fragrance. She'd discovered it when she did a fashion show in Paris five years ago. Luten said he took the essence of the white jasmine flower and made it as black as a black panther. It smelled like a fertile woman in heat, a woman who knew what she wanted and wanted it now; a sensual temptress who loved all aspects of sex. She considered it her get-lucky charm. She'd bring Bakari down, one way or another.

Sebastian kept her in good supply of Sarrasins, even though it cost a fortune. But then she'd always found men willing to go all the way to the Lutens boutique in the Palais Royal in Paris to buy it for her.

But no one was like Sebastian. She didn't need to be thinking of him right then. She inhaled the scent as she dabbed it between her breasts, and memories, erotic memories, flowed through her mind. It didn't make getting ready for another man easier.

Bare legs or garter belt? Which would he prefer? She held her white-lace garter belt in her hand and felt its slinky softness. He'd like the feel of that and it might slow him down. It had cost her a fortune in her favorite shop in Florence, but was worth every penny. After sliding it into place she pulled on sheer nylons with black seams running up the back. Very 1930s, but some fashion statements never stopped pulling in the men. The black line drawn up her long legs worked.

The garter line showed when she smoothed the dress over it, but that would only increase his anticipation. Anticipation... So much a part of her strategy.

No panties tonight. Looking directly in the mirror, she smiled at the spy with the red lipstick in place, ready to get the job done.

CHAPTER 31

At precisely seven, Sadie strode into the dining room with all the panache she'd learned on the cat walk, moving her hips in an exaggerated sway, pushing up her breasts and holding her chin high. Her lips set in a provocative pout gave her the look that had made millions. She felt his presence before she actually looked at him.

Bakari was that kind of man, a raw, alpha male who exuded energy and power. He stood and held the back of a chair for her. As she swept by him, she made sure her breast brushed his arm, which immediately made her nipple hard under the thin, silk material.

His arm stiffened and he made a small, guttural, sound low in his throat. "Nice perfume," he said as he pushed the chair in behind her.

"Thank you." Looking up at him standing above her, she narrowed her eyes for a moment like a cat ready to purr.

"It's my pleasure to please you," he said. His voice, usually commanding and hard edged, sounded softer tonight. Maybe he did know how to be a lover. He sat down across from her.

He wore a light-blue shirt, open at the neck, so that his black chest hair peeked through, and black dress pants, pressed perfectly. His olive skin glowed with energy. His black eyes held the same combustible intensity she remembered from their night together in Cairo, the intensity of a man used to getting his way. The candle light reflected on the oil he had applied in his short, black hair.

She slid off her stilettos. Should she run her foot up his inner thigh? Wander with her toes? No. Too soon. She needed to make her seduction long and slow, get as much information as she could out of him. He needed to sweat more. A lot more. "I always enjoy your company," she said.

"White wine?"

She nodded and Bakari poured. "I chose the same wine we drank in Egypt."

The maid appeared with a platter of seafood appetizers, slices of lox wrapped around cream cheese on crackers, small dishes of shrimp salad topped with a red-hot sauce, grilled scallops wrapped in prosciutto.

"No oysters?"

A slow smile spread across his face, softening his rigid features. "I don't need them."

Taking a scallop in her hand she brought it to her mouth and paused for a second, looked first at Bakari then took a bite. She chewed slowly, dramatically. Yes, her antics were textbook, but they worked. His eyes held onto her mouth.

Bakari leaned back, his olive skin flushed. "Why are you here, Sadie?"

The tone in his voice when he said her name, part simmering lust and part distrust, sent shivers up her spine. "Like I said on the phone. I wanted to see you."

"Because you broke up with that Dutch man?" The way he said "Dutch-man" and the fact that he didn't use Sebastian's name, even though he would know it amused her. Definitely the jealous type. She could work that.

"Yes. We were hot and heavy one moment and at each other's throat the next. It's over. And I'm..." she paused as if searching for her words, "looking for a man to fill my bed." She smiled at him. "And not just any man."

The right corner of Bakari's mouth twisted. "I don't know if I will ever get used to how blunt American women are."

After a slow sip of wine, she leaned towards him. "I'm a woman who knows what she wants and makes sure she gets it. I think you'll like that."

He cocked a brow. "Really. And you want me to believe you came here because you want me? I'm almost twenty years older than you."

"Don't get your socks in a knot. I'm not looking for a husband, or a meal ticket, I'm just looking for..." She raised her chin and her lips trembled. "Excitement."

He leaned back and laughed. "I can give you that." He paused. "And my secrets?"

"We all have secrets. You tell me yours and I'll tell you mine."

His eyes flowed from her face to her breasts and rested there for a moment. He picked up his wine glass and drank like a man.

"Teasing aside, I'd like to get to know you better. How is Rashida doing?"

His facial muscles froze for a second letting her glimpse his pain and then they relaxed. He put down his wine glass. "The Emerald Ankh helped. Her cancer went into remission for five and a half months. The doctors called it a miracle, but I know it was the power of the ancient magic."

"You really believe that?"

Tilting his head downward he gave her the sort of look a weary teacher gives a student. His eyes hardened and narrowed crinkling the skin around them. His lips pulled back into a half grimace and his jaw firmed.

"I'm sorry," she said. "The ankh is a beautiful relic, but I don't believe it holds any real power."

"Do you not believe in Einstein?"

Her eyebrows shot up, despite her attempt to keep a placid face. He wanted to talk physics? Now? "What has Einstein got to do with ancient Egyptian lore?"

Bakari took a deep draft of his wine and poured himself more. "According to Einstein's theory of relativity the universe is made up of energy. It can change its form, but it cannot be destroyed. The sum total of the energy always remains the same."

"Go on."

"What I am saying is that there is more to this world than what you see. People die, but their energy remains. Spirits live among us, on the edges of our reality. And, just like people, curses and blessings from the past live on. There are many mysteries in this world." His eyes didn't flinch from her face, as if her reaction to what he was saying could change things between them.

She nodded.

"The incantations and rituals of my people in ancient Egypt were strong. The Emerald Ankh has power. Believe me."

"Einstein?" She picked up another scallop and held it close to her mouth for a second before devouring it.

He flinched. "I am trying to make myself clear. My sources say you are not religious. I thought by appealing to your understanding of science, you might understand."

She tilted her head and widened her eyes. It would take a hell of lot more than equations to get her to understand this man. But maybe she didn't need to understand him, to get him to do what she wanted. She waved her hand in the air as if that would sweep away their discussion of metaphysics. "Bakari," she said in a soft voice, "I am truly sorry about Rashida. Is there anything I can do?"

Bingo. His whole body stopped for a micro-second. A normal person might not have noticed, but Sadie had learned to zone in on body reactions. She'd hit him between the eyes.

"As you probably already know, I am looking for another amulet to help her fight the cancer," he said.

She leaned forward enough to smell his expensive cologne mingled with sweat, and touched his hand. "It won't help. Why not spend your time with her instead and let her go peacefully."

He banged his other fist on the table, rattling all the dishes.

Sadie pulled her hand back. "Bakari..."

Closing his eyes for a minute, the space between them stilled. "I'm sorry. It's just that everyone keeps telling me that. Do you not understand that I love Rashida more than life itself? She is like the sun in my world. A more beautiful person you cannot find."

Sadie gritted her teeth. "It's hard to let go when you love someone."

His black eyes became even darker as he glared at her. "Don't feed me greeting card crap. Don't pretend you know how I feel. You've never been a parent." His thin mouth trembled.

Got it. "Bakari," With a soft, firm voice she aimed her words like a pointed, velvet hammer. "I doubt your wives tell you what they think. For that matter, no one does. Everyone in your world is under your command. I'm an outsider. Let me speak to you honestly."

He set his glass down. "You would have me stop looking for ways to heal her?"

"I want you to stop stealing. Sooner or later you'll get caught. From what you've told me about Rashida, she would not want you in prison. Especially...when it's because of her."

Bakari brought his fist down on the table again. "Rashida knows nothing and it will stay that way." The hardness of his eyes telegraphed an unmistakable threat. Had she gone too far?

Sadie leaned back in her chair and straightened her spine. "I would never tell Rashida what you're up to. I wouldn't want to get between the two of you—ever. You can take my word on that."

She bit her lip demurely. "But someone else might tell her." Her eyes scanned the room for a minute as if the answer might be there. "Not the CIA. They like using your business to get things done. But someone else."

Pausing, pretending to consider the point for the first time, she let a slow, smile steal across her lips. "There is your family." She needed to weaken his world as much as she could, to bring him over. "Perhaps, politics among those closest to you would loosen their lips. Jealousy destroys even the best families."

Bakari nodded. "You are a wise woman as well as a stealthy spy. Yes, of course, in my big family there are obvious and not so obvious currents of distrust and tension. Many jealousies. What can a man expect when he's had four wives and many mistresses?" He reached for his wine glass again.

"And what about your brothers?"

Bakari's shoulders tensed. He reached over and placed his hand over hers. "Sadie, do you really think you can turn me by insulting my loved ones?"

She stared back and huffed. "I had hoped so, for both our sakes." She slid her foot up the inside of his leg, playfully, but only as far as his knee.

"And that's why you're here." His lips straightened.

"That and..." She slid her foot higher. "Like I said on the phone, I'm lonely and I thought of you."

He winced when her toes neared his crotch. A warm glow spread across his face. "Sadie."

The deep gravel in his voice sent a clear message. Her next move would be pivotal. Was she ready?

The door opened and three servants in prim black uniforms entered. The first two were young women she hadn't seen before. Without making eye contact they cleared the seafood hors d'oeuvres. Elizabeth followed holding a tray bearing steaming dishes. The smell of sizzling steak and vegetables wafted through the room. Sadie's stomach gurgled and her foot dropped to the floor.

Sweat beaded on Bakari's brow, but he gave her an understanding smile.

Saved by a steak! As usual Sadie found herself relying more on serendipity than well forged plans to get the job done. Eating would cool them both down and give her time to think of her next move.

After the plates were placed in front of them and the help left, Bakari poured fresh wine. Her favorite French Cabernet Sauvignon. She kept a case of it in her New York apartment.

He raised his glass. "To new friendships."

She raised her glass and clinked his. After taking a sip she said, "I have a toast as well."

He cocked a brow. "And why am I not surprised?"

"To love." Her eyes melted into his. "It can be found in the most unexpected places."

He hesitated a moment and then chimed in, "To love." The edges of his smile trembled in their telling way, but his eyes stayed constant and commanding.

Sadie cut into her steak, a butter-soft, one inch fillet mignon cooked extra-rare, almost blue, just the way she liked it. His research on her had certainly been thorough. Feeling his eyes on her, she took her first bite. The juice of the meat exploded in her mouth. Pure heaven. She moaned.

"Glad you like it. My English cook is very good."

She looked up at him. He hadn't even touched his. "It's awesome."

"Sadie, you are an amazing woman."

Now? He wants to sweet talk me now? "Please I'm eating a steak."

He laughed and cut a piece of his own steak. He raised it to his mouth, then put it back on his plate. "No, now is good. I love your honesty, your freshness..."

"My brashness."

"Yes, but it's more than that. You come across like a ball-crusher, but underneath that warrior exterior, you have a soft and caring heart. A true heart. That is what draws me to you."

Sadie finished chewing her second mouthful. "And now?"

"Tonight, you showed me more of yourself."

Toes on the balls always works. "Uh-huh."

"I thought you were beautiful. You are even paid money to show your beauty. But tonight you showed me how..." He paused for a moment. His Adam's apple went up and down. "Sorry, I don't want to be crude. English is not my first language."

Oh boy. Here we go.

"You are all woman. The way your hips sway when you walk. Your scent. Everything about you is sensual, animal-sensual, and if I were not a mature man I would have taken you on top of this table the moment you entered."

"The table?" She looked at him and raised a brow.

His face froze and glowed. Sweat shone on his skin. She had him hook, line and sinker. He opened his mouth to say something and closed it.

Sadie rose and slowly walked over to him as she pulled out the one pin holding up her hair. Long red curls fell down to her breasts.

His eyes warmed.

Bending to whisper in his ear, her tresses fell over him. "Do you care about the cameras?"

"No." He groaned as he grabbed her right breast and the nipple hardened in his hand.

Sadie stood, slow enough that his hand had a chance to get a good feel of her body. "I would think a video of you screwing an American spy on the supper table might get you into trouble with some of your associates."

His mouth firmed and he didn't say anything for a minute. A long minute.

She leaned back down beside him, brushed her cheek against his, which was just starting to show stubble, and nibbled his ear lobe. "Can you turn the cameras off?"

He grabbed her hips and pulled her into his lap. His enormous erection pushed against her body as she settled in.

She laughed, until he brought her mouth down to his and kissed her long and deeply. She stifled a shudder and moaned like a well-priced hooker.

His other hand slid up her inner thigh, cupped her and squeezed possessively. And then he stopped. With sweat covering his face, he released her.

What was wrong? Had she made a mistake?

Panting, and with eyes, glazed over with lust, he shook his head. "Later," he said.

"No cameras?"

"I promise."

"The table?"

He gave her a roguish smile. "I'd prefer my bed."

After lifting a brow, she said, "We can start there." Slowly, she sauntered back to her seat, feeling his eyes on her body, his desire growing by the minute. His lust squeezed the air out of the room, making it hard to breathe. Bakari al-Sharif was not a man to be denied. A cold shudder ran up her spine as she took her seat.

Sadie winked at him and picked up her fork. She would have to do the horizontal mambo. How many sexual favors would it take? The man sealed his mind tighter than a sardine can and was more stubborn than a mule.

As she ate her steak, she kept her gaze on her food and wine, only looking up occasionally. Every time she did, she found him studying her as if she were a jug of water in a desert. He may as well be drooling.

Sweet Jesus. She knew that look well. Men had considered her an acquisition since she hit puberty. She smiled to herself. Yes, she would do the nasty with him, but he would pay.

Sadie put down her fork, leaned back and took a long drink of wine. Its full-bodied flavor meshed perfectly with the meat. Sighing, she pulled a hand through her hair.

He continued to stare.

"Are you going to eat?"

"I'm vegetarian," he said. "I'd rather watch you."

With as much class as she could muster, she lifted the linen napkin to her mouth and dotted her lips. "I get carried away when I have a good steak."

"I see that. I'm wondering if you get carried away at other times."

She smiled demurely. "You won't be disappointed."

He pushed his plate forward and folded his hands on the table. "Sadie, I want more from you than one night."

"Excuse me?"

"I'm attracted to you sexually. But I want more. I've never met a woman like you and I want you to be more than a..."

"One night stand?"

"Yes, exactly."

"How about two?"

He gave her that warm smile again, that came from a heart she didn't know he had. "How about we get to know each other first. If things go as well as I think they will, you could be..."

"Don't say wife. You behead your wives."

His brows shot up. "Only one. And no, you are too American to be one of my wives. I was thinking a mistress."

"The mistress of an arms-dealer? Interesting, but too dangerous in more ways than one."

"I would do everything in my power to protect you. You would have every luxury you desire. You would live like a queen. My queen."

"But I would have to share you." A little backbone would pull him further in.

"Not my heart, or even my bed. I would be monogamous if you demanded it."

"All this because you like the way I move my hips?"

"No *habibti*, though I do like your body. I'm saying that I would be willing to commit to you. The depth of your heart pulls me. With you I could have a relationship unlike any I've had before."

Relationship? A shiver stole up her spine, but she smiled and let her mouth fall into a provocative pout. With her right hand she took a tendril of her hair and curled it around her finger, keeping his attention and slowing the momentum of the moment.

"I think you'll find, as you get to know me better..." She hesitated to capture his eyes in hers. "Many things about me will intrigue you."

He opened his mouth, but before he could say anything the door of the dining room opened and Chasisi strode in. His pace was fast and assured like the commander of an army returning from a triumphant battle. Without even acknowledging her presence, he directed his attention to his brother. "Bakari, we have to talk."

CHAPTER 32

Sadie sat alone. Bakari left the dining room with his brother. Could Chasisi convince him she was up to no good? Could she do anything about it?

The French Doors had been left open a few inches letting in fresh air and the sounds of the world outside. The wind rustled through the leaves of a beech tree, and a light rain pattered on the window panes. No traffic. Bakari had chosen his neighborhood well. Although they were in the city, it felt like the country.

Considering the anger in Chasisi's face, Bakari wouldn't return right away. She looked at the half-eaten steak on her plate and did her mental calculation of calories in and calories out. The energy would do her good. Taking time, enjoying every bite of the well prepared steak and sip of the perfectly matched wine, she tried to relax, but the tension in her muscles steadily grew. Her body did that when she neared the end of an op.

How could she gain access to the office? If Bakari turned off the cameras, she could sneak out of his bed during the night and have a good look around. Risky, but doable. He might not turn off all the cameras. Or a security guy might turn them on again. He might not fall asleep. If she knew where he hid his security room, her job would be easier.

Which led her to another thought: why the hell didn't the CIA know about this house? Maybe they did and weren't in the mood for sharing. All that need-to-know baloney. She exhaled slowly. She'd have to figure it out on her own.

Elizabeth slid into the room, moving in her creepy soundless way. "Madam would you care for dessert? Perhaps a dessert wine?"

Of course Bakari knew what she liked, had made it his business to find out. Wonder what else he knew... "I'll have Madeira with dessert."

"Yes madam." The woman did a one-eighty and left. Could she be a security guard or... something? Interesting. Bakari liked to be surrounded by women, but they seemed to fall into three distinct camps: family, bedmates or... assassins.

Five minutes later the maid reappeared then once again Sadie was left alone in the big dining room. How could she get Bakari tired enough to fall into a deep sleep? She eyed the plate of cakes and pastries. She could slip him a mickey, which she carried in powder form in the base of the heel on her stiletto, but if he caught her, things would turn ugly fast. Hmm. His powerful hands could snap her neck in a minute.

She lifted her crystal glass and looked at the dark red port, swirled and sniffed it's bouquet. The Portuguese Madeira slid down her throat like warm lava and with it came a rush of good memories. Yes, a Mickey would do the trick.

Why did her drink taste more smokey than usual? Must be her mood.

Mitch had introduced her to Madeira on their first shoot together. Tucked away in a rundown chalet in the Alps, they damn near froze to death, because the organizer was too cheap to pay for decent lodgings. That first night, they huddled close together by the wood fire, as snow fell in flakes the size of ping pong balls outside and the cold bitter wind blew in between every nook and cranny.

To get their minds off their crappy situation, they took turns telling each other secrets from their past. The next day she had felt embarrassed about the whole thing. She couldn't believe she had shared with a guy friend the story of getting her first bra. At first she thought it must be the Madeira, or the cold Swiss wind. Within a week she knew it wasn't any of that. It was Mitch, his bigger than life personality and even bigger heart.

Ever since then, they made a point of drinking Madeira together. Aged for several years in wooden casks, it has an amber tone, like dried fruit, caramel and roasted nuts, and yet has a wisp of tartness. On that first night, the high alcohol content helped soothe her tired body after eight hours on their modeling gig. Not to mention the botched cat burglary the night before.

Madeira. Warm memories filled her mind with a single sip. She took another and silently toasted her absent friend. Men as friends were so much easier to deal with. Once they became lovers, life became a crap shoot. What was she thinking? Not Sebastian again. She had to put her mind back on track.

Would Bakari visit her tonight? Probably. She knocked back a second drink and headed for her room. On the way up the stairs she could hear the men arguing in the office. Clearly they weren't in agreement about something.

Her stomach clutched. She stopped and grabbed the banister beside her. It twinged again. Her gut always responded to her emotions, but this wrenching was... Oh God. Pain. Her whole stomach spasmed. She fell to her knees.

"Help," she rasped. Her voice sounded faint even to her. *No one will hear me.* Her head hit the stairway hard, and the last thing she remembered was that the carpet smelled of disinfectant.

CHAPTER 33

Bakari strode into his office with Chasisi on his heels. How dare the man interrupt his time with Sadie! Heat rushed to his cheeks and he balled his fists. How dare he! Chasisi closed the door behind them and locked it. They faced one another.

Chasisi raised his hand to caution him. "Hear me out."

"It better be good." Sweat trickled down Bakari's neck.

"I don't trust her."

"You've already told me that. Your new suspicions can wait until morning. I..."

"No," Chasisi interrupted him.

Bakari hated being interrupted. Rarely allowed it, even from his most beloved brother. He sucked in a breath, but the air didn't fully reach his lungs. His chest was too damn tight.

"She's been snooping around."

"She's a spy. What do you expect?" Had she found anything?

"Last night while you were away, someone gained access to the back stairway, and when Gahiji chased them, they escaped out the exit tunnel."

"Can he confirm it was Sadie?"

"No, he didn't get close enough. But I caught up with her outside shortly afterward."

"What was she doing?"

"She claimed to be jogging."

Bakari took a step back and turned his head to relieve the tension building in his neck. "It is possible."

Chasisi narrowed his eyes, but said nothing.

"It's in her dossier, the one you prepared for me. She runs three times a week and keeps herself in excellent physical shape." But was she running from his security men this time? That was the real question. "What about the dogs?"

"They weren't released in time to catch the person. The tunnel is old and full of smells, as is the street. They don't seem to be picking up one scent."

"So you have no proof."

Chasisi's mouth firmed and his face flushed. "Bakari wake up. She's a whoring spy who intends to stop you. She probably dreams of bringing you and your empire down. Will you let a woman, an American woman, do that?"

"How dare you insult my intelligence!" Bakari screamed.

"You're being more stubborn than a mule. She's just a woman. Have another. Have two. Have a hundred virgins. I don't care, but leave this one alone. She's deadly," Chasisi screamed back.

"I will..." Bakari stopped. What was that? "Did you hear something?"

Chasisi pulled out his mobile. "It's the security line on my phone." He held up a finger. "Yes. On it," he said to the caller.

Then he looked up at Bakari and waved for him to follow, as he ran to the door. "It's Sadie."

CHAPTER 34

*S*ounds *of swishing* and pumping and beeping machines were the first things Sadie registered when she woke. Then came the overwhelming smell of stringent chemicals, mixed with the dank smell of humanity. She opened her eyes slowly. Yup, she was in a hospital.

Bakari sat on a chair at the end of her bed. She closed her eyes again, hoping he wouldn't notice that she'd woken up. She needed to get her bearings.

Woken up? Or returned from the nearly dead. She remembered the fall, the men arguing in the office, the smell of the carpet. And then everything went black. She took an internal check on her body. Her mind worked despite a dull throb between her eyes. Possible concussion? Her eyes felt dry but her sight was fine. She wiggled her shoulders, arms and legs in turn. Everything seemed attached and functioning. But her stomach screamed for attention.

Raw, acid... pain. She knew that feeling. They had pumped her stomach.

Poison. That's why the sherry tasted a little more of oak than usual. Damn it. How could she let that happen? But who did it? Obviously not Bakari, or he wouldn't be at her bedside. She moaned dramatically and opened her eyes.

"You're awake." His voice sounded tired and sad.

"Did you poison me?"

"No." He walked to the side of her bed and took her hand. "It wasn't me."

"Then who was it?"

"My men are working on it."

She sighed. "It may have nothing to do with you."

"It happened in my home."

She screwed up her face. "A man tried to kill me in Venice last week. He committed suicide before he could be questioned. Like you, Bakari, I have enemies."

His face darkened. "I will tell Chasisi to contact people we know in Venice. I will find out who did that to you."

Sadie tilted her head. What wasn't he telling her? "You're wondering if I was the real target?" She wiggled her body up the bed and pushed the button to make the back come up and raise her into a sitting position.

He shook his head. "I don't know what to think. It doesn't make sense. I have the best security systems in place. You would be an easier target outside my house. So maybe you weren't the intended target."

"Unless someone inside your house that wants me dead."

"Who?" Anger flushed his face red in an instant. Never had she seen a person become so violently angry in such a short time.

"I'm not exactly popular in your world. There's Dead Eyes, who strangled me close to death in New York, your brother who hates me, your maid Elizabeth who is odd or..." She didn't want to say the last name.

"Dead Eyes?" His coloring faded and stabilized a solid sockeye-salmon color.

"That creepy guy you sent to the airport for me. He has the deadest eyes I've ever looked into."

Bakari nodded. "That's Gahiji. He only does what I tell him to do. He would not cross me. Ever. He'd lay down his life for me. I trust him completely." He blinked. "But I will talk to him about New York. You should have told me."

"Your brother?"

"No. We were arguing about you when it happened. He wanted me to throw you out, not end your life. We are not as barbaric as you think."

The thought of his beheaded fourth wife crossed her mind. He was definitely cruel when it suited him.

When she didn't say anything he added, "How are you feeling?"

"My head hurts and my stomach aches."

"Have some water." He poured her a glass of water from the pitcher on her side table and handed it to her. "Elizabeth may seem odd to you, but her behavior is understandable. I took her in when she was a child. She has no family and is devoted to serving mine. It's a long story. Because her early life experiences were difficult, she is different, but she is harmless. She would never hurt you."

"Maybe she has a crush on you." Sadie sipped her water, and enjoyed an avalanche of cool relief trickling down her throat.

He smiled. "Who else is on your list?" His dark eyes searched her face.

Bakari knew she was an expert liar. Did he really think he'd read her with his eyes? "The unknown man of course. Someone I don't suspect, possibly don't even know." *Who's name just might be Khalid, you idiot.* But why would his son want to kill her? Why indeed?

"That's always a possibility.

"Was there enough of the drug in my system to kill me?"

"No. Just enough to make you very sick. They either wanted to take you out of the way for a while, but not harm you permanently, or they expected you to drink more." He shifted in his seat as if something prickly stabbed his ass. "You wouldn't do it to yourself?"

He'd caught her in the middle of a swallow. Water spurted from her mouth in all directions. "Hell no!"

"I just thought maybe you wanted to get away from me."

"Aren't I still in your home?"

"No. I didn't want to deal with the wrath of the CIA. If they were to hear that you were poisoned and then contained in my house, they would come after me. You're in a local hospital."

"In a very nice private room. Thank you," she said.

He nodded. "Under the circumstances, it was the least I could do. My people are checking out all the medical staff that attends to you, and my own personal doctor is conferring with them. How are you feeling?" he asked in a softer tone this time.

Waving her hand in the air as if how she felt didn't amount to a hill of beans, she took another sip of water and swallowed it slowly. "They pumped my stomach?"

"Yes." His phone buzzed and his face reddened again. "Sadie, I must go. I have business. The man you call Dead Eyes will stand by the door. No one will harm you."

He stood and came to her side. First he took her hand. A cold reptilian touch. Then he leaned over and kissed her on her cheek. "I'm so sorry this has happened. It shames me that it happened in my own home. I apologize for not taking better care of you. Rest assured I will find out who did this to you and will show them no mercy."

A crazed glint shone in his eyes, sending a chill up her spine. Heads would roll. She'd never seen him look quite so wacko before. She was seeing the man behind the crazy shit that went down. Finally she'd seen his real face. Too bad she had to end up in the hospital. "What time is it?"

"Midnight."

Shit, she'd missed sending messages to Jeremiah and Mitch. They'd be more than worried.

A tall man with large glasses dressed in green scrubs and with a stethoscope hanging from his neck entered. He nodded at Bakari in a judicious manner and then looked at Sadie. "I'd like to talk to my patient alone," he said. His voice had a low baritone quality, that undoubtedly put his patients, especially his female patients, at ease, but something about it pricked her bull-shit meter. A little overdone somehow.

Bakari looked ruffled, like a king out of his domain. He gave her a slight bow and left the room, closing the door behind him.

"My name is Dr. Mallory." He put the blood pressure sleeve on her arm and tightened it as if punctuating his sentence. He smelled of soap; just regular old soap.

"When can I get out of here?"

He pumped up the pressure and watched the dial. "The poison was hard on your body. I'd like to keep you under observation for a while." As he stared at the scale, for longer than usual, his left hand pulled two cell-phones from his pocket and slid them under her pillow. "Your blood pressure's fine."

"Thank you."

"You took a nasty bump to your head." He traced her injury with his finger, a caring more than a professional touch. She stared at him.

"Light concussion. You'll be fine as long as you avoid bonking your head I'll give you pain killers that won't make you sleepy. Go easy on them. They could upset your stomach." He slipped a gun under her sheet. It was amazing what he could hide in his scrubs.

A doctor with a sardonic smile and interesting gifts. CIA? MI6? Some friggin acronym. Seriously sexy, whoever he was. Oh, she needed to get her head out of the gutter. Hmmm. So Bakari's people brought her to the hospital. She was admitted, had her stomach pumped and was now under observation. One of Bakari's people must have removed her weapons and phones from her body, but Bakari would have taken over and put her health as the highest priority. She rubbed her arm where the blood pressure sleeve had been.

If only she could get rid of her headache. Really hard to think with her head pounding with pain.

The doctor left. A nurse came in with pills. She took them with water and fell into a deep sleep with her hand on her gun, which she had put under her pillow.

In the middle of the night—or at least it felt like the middle of the night—her door opened and a man came in. It was a man, because he smelled so good. The door closed. No conversation. Was it a dream? She fell back to sleep.

The subdued London morning light shone through her window when she awoke. That was the first thing she noticed. The second, was the man sitting on the chair beside her hospital bed, staring at her.

CHAPTER 35

Sebastian's *sun-streaked* blond hair fell loose to his broad, athletic shoulders. The long angles on his face, lined with worry, spoke of a man who'd been suffering. As he searched her face, his blue eyes, the color of the morning sky just after dawn, filled with more emotion than could be spoken in a lifetime. His full lips trembled. "Sadie, *mijn liefje...*"

Sadie wanted to get mad at him, wanted to tell him to go away, wanted to tell him she could manage on her own, but when she opened her mouth the words wouldn't come out. She sighed.

He wore a shoulder holster with a gun. She'd never seen him with one before, but it looked good on him. Her warrior, standing guard. Warrior? How the hell did he get rid of Dead Eyes?

"What the hell took you so long?" she said, giving him a crooked smile.

He laughed. "I was busy." He smirked.

"Busy doing what?"

"Trying to forget you."

His words gripped her like a cold hand at the base of her spine. A shudder ran through her body, but she looked away pretending not to care. "How'd that go for you?"

"After a couple cases of beer and some truly fine, double-malt scotch, I was making progress, but then Mitch called."

"Mitch?"

"Said you hadn't been in contact and your cell had gone dead." He brushed his finely chiseled chin with his hand. "I got the next flight."

"Sebastian." How could she sum up her feelings?

"I know, Sadie. I know you better than you know yourself. You still care, you've always cared. It's the damn spy world that..." He swallowed. "But for right now, let's not worry about that. To hell with all of it. Just rest. I want you to get better. We can figure *us* out later."

"Us?" The certainty in his voice warmed her from the inside out. He still wanted to be together, even though she'd told him to get lost—twice, or was it three times? He wasn't the best at hearing her, but then maybe he listened with his heart and not his ears.

"There will always be an *us*, Sadie. No matter what you choose to do with your future, there will always be an *us*." Intensity built in the blueness of his eyes until they shone with energy. He had told her many times that he wasn't good at communicating, but he was wrong. He could make himself unmistakably clear.

"You mean I still have three wishes?"

A slow smile spread mischievously across his face, the boy-scout one that had disarmed her when they first met. "Have you come up with any ideas yet?"

"Ideas?" She pulled a hand through her hair. She must look a mess. "Ideas of what to do with you? That's not the problem. The problem is whittling them down to only three."

He laughed, his deep, hearty laugh, and for a moment it seemed like they'd got their old couple-thing back; the Sadie and Sebastian dynamite lovers thing; the we don't care what the rest of the world is doing as long as we're together thing; the wake up in the morning and wish the night had never ended thing.

"Let's see if I can help. Do any of them involve hospital beds?" He stood up and moved towards her, towering above her bed with his six and a half feet of solid muscle.

"Not here." Although... She really did want to jump his bones; not just for the pure erotic thrill of it—and that would be mighty fine—but for that deep intimacy she felt every time they made love.

"We could get a hotel room." He reached down and pushed curls away from her face with the most tender of touches. "I could play doctor."

"What did you do with Dead Eyes?"

He smiled as he shrugged. "Last I saw him an Interpol officer with a thick Scottish accent was marching him down the hallway. Something about his passport."

Their friend Seamus. She laughed at the thought of the two men together, the evil Arab henchman spitting venom and the Celtic warrior citing the laws of the land and a pile of bullshit. She laughed, then stopped because it hurt her throat too much. The lining of her esophagus felt like it was ripped apart and on fire.

Sebastian winced. His eyes softened to a mellow hue, dripping with compassion. "How do you feel?"

Watching him respond to her pain gave her heart another squeeze. She took a deep breath and let it out slowly. "I don't know what part of me hurts more. My throat feels like someone lit a fire in it, and my head feels like sumo wrestlers are trying to tango in it."

He laughed low in his throat as he stroked her hair with his gentle touch. "Just another day at the office. On a scale of one to ten?"

"Five."

That mischievous glint in his eye came back, the one she teased him about, that made him look like a giant leprechaun. "Then let's get that hotel room."

CHAPTER 36

*T*hey left the hospital through a back exit, walked two blocks and grabbed a cab. Sadie, wearing a trench coat Sebastian had brought her and hospital slippers, slid into the back seat quickly. Sebastian followed.

"Where to?" The driver, a dark-skinned man with spiky hair and a nose ring, looked at them in the rear view mirror with clouded-over eyes as if he wanted his shift over yesterday.

Sadie nudged Sebastian with her elbow and took the lead. "Look, I'm hiding from my husband. I want a nice hotel, off the radar, if you know what I mean. There's an extra hundred euro for you if you totally forget ever meeting us." Sebastian would have that in his pocket.

The driver's eyes came alive and he raised a brow. "Two hundred and I'll take you to the finest back street lover's den I know. And no one will be the wiser."

Sadie opened her mouth to object, but Sebastian spoke. "Deal." He grabbed Sadie`s hand and held it for the rest of the journey, looking out the window and saying nothing.

The morning light, subdued by clouds and drizzle, etched the city landscape. People scurried in every direction, pursuing their lives. In Amsterdam the morning commuters would be riding on bicycles, giving big hellos to their friends as they passed. In New York, people would be bobbing their heads at acquaintances as they rushed for the subway with a hot coffee in their hands. And in Venice... Ah, in Venice the people would be knocking back espressos and enjoying delicate pastries at their favorite café. They would speak in rapid Italian with their hands as much as their mouths. Reflecting off the moody, blue waters of the Grand Canal the morning light would be doing its magic. But being in wet London with Sebastian felt mighty fine.

Leaning into his body, soaking in his warmth, his strength, his manliness, she listened to his heart-beat, slow and steady. Maybe it wasn't too late to take back what they'd lost.

Ten minutes later they were dropped off at a boutique hotel. The small entrance had no footmen or security. Perfect.

On the way up in the elevator, Sebastian pulled Sadie into his arms and they kissed long hard and deep. Her body lit on fire, but her mind hit the pause button.

The longer they were together, the harder it would be to pull apart. He couldn't get in the way of nailing Bakari. Her mind screamed "impossible!" Did she really think she could be a spy and have a relationship with a man? Who was she kidding?

But then he kissed her on her sweet spot, the one just behind her ear. That one. His erection pushed against her. She gasped as desire and love flowed through her with the power of a tidal wave. Her mind ceased functioning.

**

Sebastian's hands trembled as he held Sadie in his arms. He wanted this woman more than anything in the world. But she kept pushing him away, denying what they had, telling him it was over... when they were just beginning. If she'd only listen to him. The heady smell of her perfume burned in his nostrils. Her soft breasts pushed against his chest. Her breathing hitched as he leaned in for another kiss. If they made love one more time, maybe that would take them back to where they'd been, to that sense of togetherness that couldn't be touched by anything in the fucking world. And didn't fall apart.

She tasted like honey and magic. Memories of their sex life flooded into his system, making him want her even more. Sadie did that to him. She was more than a lover, more like an addiction. He whispered in her ear, "Give us a chance, Sadie. One more chance." He wanted to make love to her, push into her warmth, touch her deeply in her body and soul.

She moaned deep in her throat.

**

The room smelled like hotel rooms everywhere, cleaning fluids mingling with the body odors of the masses. But she didn't care how it looked or how it smelled. All she cared about was Sebastian. She undid the buttons of her coat and it fell to the floor. He locked the door with a dead bolt.

Turning to face him, she smiled. He lifted his chin and strode over to her, scooping her into his enormous arms, pulling her to him, so close she could feel his heart beat. Not only was he technically the best lover she'd ever had, he was the most enthusiastic. Pure lust burned through her veins. Nothing felt better than his embrace. Nothing—in the world. But...

"Sebastian?"

He groaned. "I don't want to talk." He lifted her and took her mouth with his in a long passionate kiss that sent shivering currents of passion through her body. She twisted her legs around him, bringing his erection closer to her. She pushed into him. Oh god, how she wanted him, needed him. He felt so good... tasted so good.

Wait. What was she doing? She couldn't keep playing with him, knowing that their relationship was impossible. It wouldn't be right to let his... their... their feelings deepen. She needed to be more... mature. Or something.

Carefully he placed her on the bed. Towering above her, he undid his shirt and threw it on the floor. She bit her bottom lip. His broad, muscular chest, sculpted like a Greek god, made her want to whimper. He ripped off his pants. His erection was truly magnificent.

For a minute he stood looking at her, but his expression wasn't that of a confident lover. Shadows of doubt clouded his eyes, and his lips trlembled. Gone was the sexy bad-boy grin she'd become used to before they made love; the one that whispered he had many plans for her; the one that never failed to make her wet, even just thinking about it. Because Sebastian always delivered.

Unable to stand the anticipation any longer, she reached for him, wanting to comfort him like an old friend, wanting to fuck him like a new lover and wanting to steady herself in an emotional world that refused to make sense.

He took her hand in his and looked into her eyes. But he made no move. Damn it. He always made a move. And move... and move... and move... But not this time.

"Touch me," she said, hearing the husky need in her own voice. "I need you to touch me." *Make me feel whole. Make me feel like there's an us again. Make me feel.*

Releasing her hand, he lay down beside her and propped himself up on one arm. He pushed the hair away from her face and leaned in for a kiss. His lips were gentle at first, then more intense as his tongue entwined with hers. It felt good to be together... to play, but she wanted more from him, much more. She reached for his penis and he groaned.

His hand slid down her body tracing first her breast and then heading for her center. His touch lit her on fire and an unbearable ache, low in her belly, tightened like a drum. His thumb stroked her clit as one of his fingers sank into her vagina and played.

Oh, how she missed this. How she missed him. She moaned as she pressed her hips up to meet his hand. More. She wanted more. Firmly he stroked her nub as his finger caressed the walls of her vagina with a rhythm that drove her wild. Just when she thought she couldn't hold on for one more minute, his finger found her spot and she exploded, screaming out as the tension in her body shattered into a million pieces of ecstasy.

Her orgasm ripping apart not only her body's control, but her heart's.

He nuzzled her neck as he rolled on top of her. "I love you," he whispered.

"I know," she whispered back.

Entering her softly, he filled her with his strength, like a lion claiming his lioness. This must be what heaven felt like. Sex with Sebastian took her to a whole new dimension. They moved together in unison to a rhythm all their own.

He came in one hard thrust and she wrapped her legs around him to bring him in as close as she could, and her body exploded in pleasure. He shuddered as he lay entwined in her legs.

Spent and satisfied they held one another for a long time.

Could she ever really let Sebastian go?

"Hey, Studly, how do you feel about puppies?"

CHAPTER 37

*K**halid walked slowly* through his father's neighborhood. *Why did I ever think coming to London would be a good idea?* There were few people on the street and lots of weird shaped shrubbery. A young woman pushed a baby stroller neared him. She had nice boobs, but she didn't make eye contact.

Wandering back to the house, he continued to take inventory of the area, but nothing caught his interest, nothing out of the ordinary. Avoiding the weird maid-in-black with the suspicious eyes, he headed for his room. His father had gone to the hospital with Sadie. It seemed the man was always surrounded by drama.

Once inside his room he laid out his crystals, tarot cards, candle and incense on the desk. He pulled out his wand, and held it in his hand feeling its energy pulsate from the spirit world into him. Yes, this was what he needed to do.

He lit the candle and the incense and looked back at the door. He had locked it, but would that be enough? He couldn't be disturbed in the middle of conjuring the spirits, so he pushed a lounge chair against it. Nothing this simple would keep the likes of his uncle Chasisi or his henchmen out, but it would stop the prying eyes of the stupid maid who kept offering weak tea and biscuits.

Sitting in the chair by the desk, he let memories of his childhood flood through him as the sensual smell of kyphi grew stronger: cinnamon, honey and wine. He indulged in his past, then said a silent protection prayer.

What he was about to do would take him beyond any protection, but the prayer was a habit. He had been told over and over again that when you allow evil spirits inside you, they take over. He could no longer avoid evil. His only hope was to control it.

Images of his mother and his fear flowed through him like water through a drain-pipe, until his mind found its peace in the center of the storm. He gained first an emptiness; then from that emptiness a majestic fullness so grand he could barely contain it. Exhaling slowly he felt eternity in his being, all that was and all that will be. He entered into that feeling like a child opening a door to the outside world, and basked in the light of the universe. His chest expanded. His scalp tingled. He had been to the threshold of this world many times before, but never like this. Never had he felt so fucking powerful. Yes, he concluded, his time had come.

Lifting his wand, he made an eternity symbol in the air. "Demon-goddess, darkness of light, I call on you. Show me the way."

The light dimmed as a dark smoke that smelled like burning tires filled his consciousness. A bitter taste burned his lips and his senses heightened in fear. A deep, guttural voice spoke, "Let me in. I will show you the way."

A shuddering shiver ran deep inside him. Part of him wanted to run... to hide. Part wanted to turn back to the light, to beg for sanctuary. After all, doesn't the light of the universe always forgive? Or is that just a myth for suckers?

As these thoughts and fears battled in his mind, he tried to swallow, but no spit remained in his mouth. His whole body-mind-and-soul squished up against a mirror of darkness, like a black hole, without dimension, without end... pulling at the sinews of his being. Sour sweat poured from his skin soaking into his clothes.

His smell accosted his nostrils. He could barely breathe. From some unfathomable place deep within came a thin voice, he barely recognized as his own. "You have my permission."

The black smoke coalesced into the form of Ammit the Devourer, in her hot woman form, naked except for her arcane tattoos. Her other-worldly, orange eyes bored through his, piercing through his body... into his lost soul. "You want to be the most powerful sorcerer in the world. You need to get the scarab."

"What about the woman..."

"She's a detail in the background of your life. Static, nothing more. Ignore the bitch. Get the scarab." The hissing of her voice made the hair all over his body stand.

"You make it sound so easy, but I'm not a soldier, I am a seer."

The she-demon groaned deep in her throat and the air rumbled like an earthquake. Her stench intensified. "You are my hands and feet on earth. Trust that I am behind you. Trust my power. Our power."

Did he now have her demonic energy behind him? He already knew this, but he didn't believe it until now. Brushing at the cold sweat flowing down my forehead into his eyes, he tried to swallow again, but the fires of hell had left it too dry.

"Demon. Shall I call you that? Or what should I call you?"

An odd chortling sound came from her perfectly shaped lips. "I have had many names since the dawn of time. Your ancestors called me Ammit. But, that sounds odd now. I like to keep up with the times. You may call me the Darkness of the Night, the Evilest of the Evil, the End of All Hope... or you can simply me 'Soul-Eater.'"

She laughed again. "Has a ring to it, don't you think?" A long, reptilian tongue flashed out and licked her wide lips slurping hideously. The hair on the nape of his neck bristled. Red spittle dripped to the ground from her mouth. The blood of her victims?

Another soul-ripping shiver coursed through his body. His stomach sank to his knees. "Soul-Eater, tell me what to do. I will do your bidding, but I need your help."

"Aaaaah, a willing soldier. I like that." Her eyes blazed. "Yes, I think you will do nicely."

He waited for her to say more, but she strode around the room checking everything out.

She stopped directly in front of him, her face within inches of his. "You must follow your father's plans carefully. Help him. Let him steal the treasure. Then take it, by any means. Kill him if you have to. That scarab will seal your fate."

"The woman?"

"Again with the woman! She doesn't matter. Fuck her if you want. Kill her if you want. But don't bother me about a mere mortal with goodness in her heart." She trembled when she said the word goodness. Then her mouth twisted into an ugly grin.

"If you must know, the key to getting the wench to do what you want is to enter her dreams. That's what your mother did. The woman has a recurring nightmare that takes place in Africa. It makes her particularly vulnerable, because her emotions open up when she sees a baby about to be sacrificed. You enter then, and you can feed on her fear and anxiety. You can bend her will and she won't even know it."

Visit her in a nightmare? Intriguing. He still couldn't let it go. He had to let the soul-eater know how dangerous Sadie was on this plane. "She has her own power. She could stop my father."

The Soul-Eater raised her head. "Yes, the woman will try to do that, but Bakari al-Sharif will not be stopped by a pretty face. He will bend every rule in the universe to acquire the power he needs. Like son, like father." She chortled again. More blood spittle fell on his shoes.

Khalid resisted jumping back. He was part of her world now, a minion of the forces of darkness. He must accept all aspects of it, if he were to use its power. "Where shall I take the scarab?"

"You will need to create your own sanctuary, a place where you can practice your skills and grow stronger; a place the forces of light will have difficulty finding. I would suggest Egypt, because it is my motherland, but for you Amsterdam would be better. You know the city and its people. Find a place to hide and conjure." She shuffled her feet and clawed the floor. "But..."

Khalid stopped breathing, waiting for her to say more.

"There could be a complication."

"What?"

The Soul-Eater nodded her massive head from side to side, stomped her foot and vanished. The smoke that flooded the room dissipated in seconds and Khalid stared at empty space. Only a few drops of blood on his shoe were left to remind him of what had just happened.

His nose felt wet and he touched it. Blood flowed down his fingers and pooled on his shoes mixing with the demon's blood. *What the fuck?*

CHAPTER 38

Sadie snuck out of bed at first light. Sebastian caught up with her in the shower and their lovemaking started all over again.

A couple hours later, she lay sated in his arms back on the bed. "Sebastian I need to get going."

He grumbled.

"I have a job to do."

More grumbles.

"Bakari plans to steal a priceless Egyptian relic from Highclere castle. I have to stop him."

He grumbled a third time and propped himself up on one of his elbows. "And you're the only one who can stop him?"

She grumbled. Her turn.

"Sadie, listen to me. Let the locals take care of it."

"They're involved, but no one has gotten as close to Bakari as me. I have the best chance of stopping him, or, at the very least, finding out his plans so someone else can stop him."

"Okay, so let me get this straight. You're going back to that geiten neuker. You'll bat your eyelashes and expect him to tell you everything.?" Goat fucker was Sebastian's favorite name for Bakari.

"Not exactly, but sort of."

Sebastian rolled on his back away from her.

"I have his ear. He listens to me. He…"

"Wants to fuck you."

"Yes, but that's beside the point."

"Not to me."

"Sebastian, I can handle him. I know what makes his heart tick. I'm half-way to convincing him to give up on this." That was a bit of a stretch, but that's where she wanted to be.

"Handle. That's my concern. Who exactly is handling who? I don't want his hands on you."

"I can take care of myself."

"Someone poisoned you."

"It wasn't him. He doesn't want to hurt me."

"Not yet, but Sadie…" He paused. "He's an evil son of a bitch. He already knows you used to work with the CIA. Once he figures out you're playing him again, he'll kill you. The man shows no mercy."

"I know. I know. He doesn't understand the concept. You don't have to tell me this. I understand Bakari al-Sharif."

"Then why?"

"There's a lot you don't know about the man. I told you, the only reason he stole the amulets before was that he wanted to save his dying daughter. Her health did improve, but it's declining again. He really believes King Tut's scarab will help her. The only thing that's important to Bakari is his family. Rashida is his favorite daughter. He would do anything for her."

"I don't give a fuck."

"But I do. I'm trained to find the weakness in people. I know his and I know how to use it."

"So the guy has a glimmer of love in his stone heart. So what? He's an asshole who puts guns in the hands of children. He's volatile and unpredictable. Walks around like a fucking grenade with its pin half pulled." He exhaled noisily. "And, god dammit, he wants to screw you."

Back to that. "Sebastian, I love you. Isn't that enough."

"Fuck, no."

"I've got to go. If you're still around when my op's over we can hook up again. But in the meantime, stay out of my way." She got up to take another shower but stopped herself. Sebastian would join her again and they didn't have any time left for play. She started hunting for clothes. "Oh shit, I forgot I came in a hospital nightgown."

Sebastian said nothing.

She gave him her narrowed-eyed, get-over-it look.

Ignoring her, he stared at the ceiling. His cheeks flamed red. A sheen of sweat from their love making lingered on his crinkled brow.

"I have clothes at Bakari's house. I'll just have to arrive as-is."

"In pajamas?" He thumped his hand on the bed and sat up. "Do you even have a plan?"

"I think better when I'm moving. I'll head over, reinsert myself into his household, and figure out things from there."

Sebastian shook his head. His long sun-kissed blond hair looked wild in the morning light. She wanted to pull her hands through it, wanted to hold him close again, wanted to feel him inside her. One more time. Damn the man got under her skin. His eyes, bluer than blue, implored her to stop.

But she couldn't.

**

Twenty minutes later a taxi dropped her off in front of Bakari's London home. Elizabeth greeted her at the door with a dour expression, even more sour than the one she wore the day before, as if Sadie was yesterday's bad news. It hadn't bothered her to drive in the taxi in her hospital gown, but when this woman gave her the once-over, she felt naked to the core. With one hand she held the open back of the nightie closed and straightened her shoulders.

Bakari walked forward to meet her. Chasisi watched from the open entrance of the office.

"We've been looking for you." Bakari's voice held concern, not anger. That was a good thing. The maid slid away.

"I didn't feel safe in the hospital. I don't know who poisoned me or why. So I left and stayed with a friend."

"Sebastian Wilde, your lover."

"Sebastian Wilde, my *former* lover. I knew I could trust him."

"You can trust *me*." The word "me" echoed in the foyer with a threatening force.

She put up her hand to stop him. "I know I can trust you, Bakari, but someone in your household tried to kill me. I don't feel safe here."

"So why did you come back?" Chasisi's voice crossed the foyer

Sadie ignored Chasisi and kept her eyes on Bakari. "I wanted to fly straight to New York, but my passport and clothes are here. And..." How could she word this and make it sound real? "I didn't want to leave without seeing you."

A glint of light slid across Bakari's dark eyes. The fine muscles in his face relaxed.

Elizabeth reappeared with a white cotton robe folded over one arm. She handed it to Sadie. "I've asked the cook to put the kettle on."

"Thank you." Sadie released the back of her gown and slid the garment on. Pulling it tight with the belt, she gave Bakari an appreciative smile. Warm and clothed again. See, her plan was working.

CHAPTER 39

"I 'll take my tea in my room," Sadie said to Elizabeth. Turning to Bakari she added, "I need to sort myself out."

He nodded like a gentleman. "Stay and get some rest. You will be safe here and I will visit you later."

Chasisi, still standing by the office, glared at her. If glares were knives, his was a machete. With as much grace as she could muster in bare feet and a borrowed housecoat, she ascended the stairs. Near the top she stopped on the spot where she'd fallen the day before. The visceral memories flooded back. Nausea, weak knees... blackness. No hint of who'd done the poisoning, though. No memory of anyone watching. She continued up the stairway.

Once inside her room she took a deep breath. Was Bakari's weird son still hanging about? Had he poisoned her? Khalid definitely acted as if he had a few missing synapses in his head, but how would you expect a young man with Bakari's blood to behave? Many believed his mother to be a sorceress descended from a long line of adepts who followed ancient

Egyptian rites and rituals. A shiver stole up her spine. The sooner she could end this op, the better. There was something seriously creepy about dealing with Egyptian amulets.

The tea arrived. She lounged in a chair by the window, smelled the drink, tasted it and then gulped it down. The tray of small sandwiches and sweets she ignored. It could still be Elizabeth or the cook. Besides she didn't need the empty calories. There'd be time for eating later. Scanning the room she saw a new camera on the wall. Great.

Bakari didn't arrive, which surprised her. Did he have too many plans to make? She took a quick shower and put on a low-cut, black dress. With her make-up in place, she headed back downstairs.

She stopped at the bottom. Male voices came through the closed door of the office. She listened for a couple minutes. At least three men. The front door of the house opened and Khalid entered. He smelled of weed, but his body didn't have a relaxed stoned look. He glanced her way, nodded then shifted his eyes away, as if eye contact with her was forbidden. She upgraded him to seriously weird.

"I heard you were poisoned," he said.

Hello to you too. "Would you know something about that?"

His mouth turned up into an insipid smile and he shrugged. "Weird shit happens around my father."

As if on cue, the office door opened and Bakari strode out with all the majesty of a king returning to his court. Khalid watched his father, not like a devoted son, more like an adversary waiting his turn to rule. Interesting dynamics.

"My brother Chasisi is trying to find who poisoned you." His olive colored skin pinked. "He thinks it may have something to do with that renegade group of Egyptians who have sworn an oath to protect the Emerald Tablets. I've never heard of them."

A shiver scaled her spine. She nodded. "The KOTL, the Keepers of the Light. A possibility."

"You don't look surprised."

"As a spy I have made many enemies."

"You don't live a safe life."

She laughed. "Safe is boring." Giving him as provocative a look as she could muster with Khalid in the room she closed the distance between them.

"He says they are not to be ignored."

"I never ignore bad boys." She smiled. Oh that sounded cheesy, but given the dull ache that remained in her head it was the best she could do.

Khalid cleared his throat. "I don't think you two need me." He walked up the stairs.

Bakari reached for her arm. The soft touch, meant to comfort, sent a cold chill into her heart like an arrow from Satan's bow. "Come into my office and we'll talk to my security people. They have questions for you."

Yes, the office. She wanted to dance, but kept a solemn expression as she let him lead her into his sanctuary. Attached to the dangling earrings she had been wearing since she arrived in London was a bug. Her company cell-phone remained strapped to her inner thigh. Things might work out after all.

Chasisi, Dead Eyes and another man stood when they entered the room. The unknown man looked to be in his early twenties. He had military-short black hair and Mediterranean coloring. He dressed in black and wore combat boots. Must be one of the foot soldiers.

Sadie walked towards Chasisi and offered her hand with a forced smile worthy of a cheap magazine cover. "Good to see you again."

Dead Eyes grunted and sat.

Chasisi made a small bow and sat. He crossed his long legs.

She took her hand back and felt her smile widen. "I like a man who shows his feelings."

Chasisi lit a cigarillo and blew smoke into the air. The soldier lowered himself with regimental dignity into the chair beside him and looked at the floor.

Cozy. Looking at the soldier-guy she said, "I'm Sadie Stewart, the poison victim."

He nodded, looked at her briefly then returned his gaze to the floor.

Bakari ushered her to a chair beside his brother. "You'll have to excuse the grimness of my men. They are extremely good at what they do and yet my security has been breached twice in twenty-four hours."

"Twice? Was someone else poisoned?"

"No." Bakari searched her face.

She held every tiny muscle in her body under control to keep an innocent look in place, knowing that his bull-shit meter was unparalleled. "What then?"

"You don't have to worry about that."

"Are you sure? I'm really not in the mood for dying. Getting poisoned really sucked." She turned and bored her eyes into Chasisi. "Can't you do a better job?"

All eyes turned to the head of security, and to see how he'd react to her brazen question. Sadie pretended to adjust her right earring as she slipped a bug onto her finger and into her hand. Step one—achieved.

Chasisi's lips curled. "Rest assured, madam, you will not be poisoned again."

She smiled at the fact that he didn't say she wouldn't be killed. Only that it wouldn't be poison. Turning her anger to Dead Eyes she stood and said, "And what about you? Can't you do something?"

All eyes turned to the henchman as she slid the bug under the edge of Bakari's table and threw up her hands in disgust. Step two—done.

Old Dead Eyes grunted. This one, lower in tone. He had a whole grunt vocabulary.

Sadie sat and gave Bakari a doe-eyed look. "I don't know how I can help you. I told the police everything I know. After dinner I walked up the stairs, had a sudden, violent stomach cramp, fell and then everything went black."

Chasisi blew more toxic smoke into the air. "What can you tell us about KOTL?

"Not much." She grimaced.

"One of their assassins tried to kill you a week ago, and you know nothing about them? Weren't your friends at the CIA concerned?"

"Like I told Bakari, I have enemies. There's little information available about the assassin or his group." She shook her hair behind her shoulders. "For now, I consider it a dead end." She sighed. "Well…" She paused for drama, "More than that really. I consider it a warning. Someone out there wants me dead." It wouldn't hurt to play the helpless female. Judging by Bakari's body language, especially the way his face softened. He was eating it up.

Chasisi—not so much. He blew more smoke in the air. "The man swallowed cyanide." His tone was as matter-of-fact.

"Have you learned more?" Her throat started to close as it did when danger neared. Perhaps they had better intel than the Venice police and the CIA.

"Not yet. I want to know why that group wants to kill you."

"Me too. Trust me—me too."

"Did you take something from them?"

"Not to my knowledge. I didn't even know they existed until after the attack. I sent a picture of the assailant to an old friend at the CIA and he told me about the man's connection with KOTL."

"Why do they think it happened?"

"No one has a clue. I figure they're just another group of wing-nuts living in the shadows and somehow I pissed them off. Unless..." Oh shit, she hadn't thought of that.

"Unless what?" Bakari said.

"Unless they wanted to kill me to get back at you." A bit of a leap, but not beyond possibility.

Bakari's mouth flattened and he looked at Chasisi. "Is that possible? Would stealing amulets upset them?"

Chasisi blew more smoke into the air. "To my knowledge the group exists for one purpose and one purpose only, to protect the Emerald Tablets. While some of them may curse you for stealing Egyptian treasure, I don't think they would act on it. It's not what they do."

"Where the hell are these green tablets?" Sadie asked.

Chasisi shrugged. "I don't believe they exist. Like you, I think they are a group of—what did you call them?—wing-nuts." He exhaled more smoke. "But wing-nuts can kill. The power of faith and the sense of belonging that a cult gives its members cannot be underestimated. Someone could be orchestrating your death through this group."

Bakari leaned back in his chair. "Why can't you find out more about them?"

"They take an oath, swearing they'll die before they talk. I got my information from a crooked Venetian policeman, not from the back alleys of Egypt."

Sadie winced. None of this was making sense. "You're thinking that one of their operatives penetrated your security and attempted to kill me? Once or maybe even twice?"

Dead Eyes gave her his darkest look.

Chasisi mulled over her words, blowing more smoke into the air. "That's my best guess."

Bakari pounded the table with his fist. "Find him and kill him."

"Or her." Chasisi said. "We've vetted all the staff. The poison was in the Madeira. They must have known she would choose it and you would not, which means they know things about both of you. That is my only clue. Nothing else was contaminated."

"So who had access to my liquor cabinet?" Sweat beaded on Bakari's brow. "I thought our staff controlled all our food and drink."

"They do, but someone slipped poison into the bottle. Elizabeth heard Sadie fall and ran to the dining room, but it was too late. Sadie was unconscious on the stairs."

Sadie stretched her neck. "What about your CCTV cameras?"

"The kitchen one…" Chasisi hesitated, "malfunctioned. None of the others show anything unusual."

Sadie gave Bakari a hard look. "Are all your personnel really above reproach?"

Bakari held her stare.

Chasisi answered. "On my life, I swear they have all been vetted and have sworn allegiance to the family. We pay for loyalty."

"And threaten them on the side," she added, breaking the eye-lock with Bakari to look at Chasisi.

"Of course." Chasisi's smile would look good on a snake. No, a snake would shed it. It looked so evil and so... arrogant, in a slimier than slime way. It messed with her head. Or tried to.

Bakari waved his hand to dismiss this tangent of the discussion. "None the less, Sadie was poisoned in my home."

"What about him?" Sadie said pointing at Dead Eyes.

The henchman twisted his face her way. His eyes bulged out of his head and twitched with a malicious light. His jaw clenched. His cheeks colored. Sweat ran down his face. "I didn't do it."

Wow, a whole sentence! "You have the run of the house. I assume you have the intelligence. And you hate me."

Bakari leaned back and smiled, as if humored by the play of children. "No, Sadie. Not Gahiji."

"It's possible."

"First of all, Gahiji obeys all my orders. One of which is to protect you while you are in my home. Second, if Gahiji decided to kill you, he'd never use poison. His methods are…" Bakari hesitated, "shall we say more of the flesh and blood variety."

Chasisi laughed. "Much more blood." A grim smile stayed on his face. Asshole

Great. Let's all take a mental picture of what Dead Eyes would like to do with me, if he had the chance. "Elizabeth?"

All four men shook their heads.

"Definitely not," said Bakari in the severest of tones.

There had to be a lot more to her story. She tilted her head and cocked a brow.

He took a moment as if he wasn't sure he wanted to tell her more about the maid, then he said, "I rescued her from… shall we say an ugly situation."

"Ugly?" Okay.

"She would die before she would betray me."

"You surround yourself with loyal people."

"Of course. Don't you?"

"Then why has your security been breached?" Slowly, she tossed her hair over her shoulder. Bakari's eyes took in her shoulder then traveled to her breasts. She gave him a quick, seductive smile.

Chasisi broke his mood. "There weren't any problems until an American spy came into the house."

She glanced his way. "I could leave," she said.

Chasisi smiled like a Cheshire cat. Bakari sat up straight. "You are my guest. This is my house. I won't have you chased out."

"It might be safer for her elsewhere," Chasisi said in a razor-sharp voice. He'd be damn good in a spaghetti Western. "Have you thought of that?"

She waited, expecting Bakari to answer, but silence tumbled into the room and extended longer than she'd anticipated. Her scalp tingled, but she remained stoically calm.

Warring emotions played across Bakari's face. "Chasisi is right. Until I know who breached our security system, you are safer elsewhere."

Sadie stood.

"I will see that you have a nice room in your favorite hotel."

She leaned over the desk and put her hand on his. "No need Bakari. Chasisi is right. I am being hunted. I'll find a safe place to figure things out."

"Sadie..." Bakari took her hand in his and stood to face her.

"Bakari, we will find our time. It's just not now."

Anger rippled across the muscles of his face like a dark wave, clouding his eyes. "When I find the men tracking you, they will die." The fury in his voice stiffened her backbone. He squeezed her hand. "Slowly."

She swallowed and smiled, but it wasn't easy. Her throat had tightened and become as dry as the desert. Some women get flowers. The image of a pile of brutally murdered men left at her feet didn't warm the cockles of her heart.

It was meant to be a testament of his affection. One she needed to answer accordingly. Sheesh. Flirting with arms-dealers could really could get nasty. What could she say? She wanted the bodies of her enemies left in small pieces for the dogs? Her gut twisted. Humor couldn't shake the feelings that sank into her with his words.

In her heart, she felt a warmth she could not deny. When a man is willing to kill to protect you, to commit the greatest of crimes, the greatest of sins, for you... it changes things. She'd once thought Bakari's magnetism to be a mixture of his exotic charm and bad-guy macho crap, but it was more. Bakari had a big heart and he would do anything, at any cost to himself, for those he loved.

To be loved by such a man would be interesting... Sadie stopped her thought right there.

She gave him as warm a look as she could manage. "Bakari, before I go..." She let her voice trail off and held his dark gaze.

"Yes."

"I have to ask you, beg you, one more time, to reconsider what you're doing. No relic has the power to extend Rashida's life. Spend what time she has left with her. Be together. Honor her with your presence, not your crimes. The amulets belong in a museum."

Chasisi put his cigarillo to his side. "Listen to the woman, Bakari. Both you and Rashida are safer without the relics."

"Why can't you understand? Why can't anyone understand? I can't sit and watch my daughter die. I can't. I must do whatever I can to save her. My destiny is sealed." His anger spoke louder than his words.

Chasisi rose slowly and headed for the door with his distinctive limp. "Subborn old goat."

Sadie couldn't help smiling. They may be serious bad-guys, but they were also brothers. Dead Eyes and the young man headed for the door. Sadie held her ground.

"Lock the door on your way out," Bakari said in a steady voice as his eyes swept over Sadie's body like a lover's hand.

CHAPTER 40

After her interlude with Bakari, Sadie threw on her clothes and took a cab to the grand entrance of Hyde Park. His sweat had dried on her body. His smell clung to her nostrils. The deed was done.

Part of her wanted to get away more than anything in the world, preferably to another universe, while another questioned, yet again, her mission. Bakari held crazy old ideas, but all he really wanted to do was protect his daughter. Was that so bad?

Who the hell has the right to own ancient Egyptian amulets anyway? The British aristocracy? Dusty museums? Who?

Oh shit. She had forgotten to turn her feelings off when her clothes fell to the floor. And then there was the matter of him not using a condom. *Shit, shit, shit.*

While the car battled the busy traffic she sent a text to Reggie, her friend at MI5. He replied that he was out of the country, but would get his office to send another operative to meet her inside the Ionic columns of the entrance. A woman about her age with long blond hair pulled up into a classic French twist approached her with a welcoming smile. She had a decidedly pointed nose holding up large, square glasses, and dressed like an executive secretary. With a highbrow English accent that would sound good in any aristocrat's home, the woman said, "A good time to visit London."

"Never better," Sadie replied. "The sound of the pigeons cooing is mesmerizing." *Who the hell thinks up these lines?*

The woman took her by the elbow and ushered her back out to the street at a fast clip. "My name is Eleanor. I'll take you to the house." No doubt a safe house.

Her car was small, but fast. As they weaved through traffic, in a circuitous route, Sadie sent a text to Jeremiah on her new cell-phone, updating him on her situation. She ended with, "Let me know if you get anything interesting from the bug."

It was noon by the time they reached their destination, a non-descript, brick townhouse in a run-down residential area that looked like the home of not just the poor, but the criminal. Eleanor handed her a key and a business card, which read, "Eleanor Riggs, Management Consultant. Let me manage you."

Eleanor checked her rear view mirror one more time. "Everything you need is inside. Text me if you need help. It's been a pleasure to meet Mata Hari in person." Her eyes twinkled as her accent dropped to something that sounded more Australian than British.

Sadie nodded and exited the car. Mata Hari. It wasn't the first time she regretted being given that code name. It left way too much to live up to.

Once inside she locked the door and turned on the electronic locks and sensors set up on the wall. Then she cased the place. On the entrance floor was a small living room with worn furniture and an electric fireplace, a basic kitchen with three mousetraps, a line of mouse turds and a fridge stocked with milk, eggs and bread. As she climbed the stairs covered in 1970s-era shag carpet, she could hear the neighbors in the next house arguing, but couldn't make out the words. On the second floor were two bedrooms and a bathroom that smelled of mildew. One bedroom had been decorated for a young girl, the other for the girl's parents. On the child's bed sat a fat marmalade cat who gave her a bemused look, as if he were the master spy of the house.

"You could at least catch the mice," she said to him.

He growled, arched his back and hissed at her. Not her best day. She turned and walked into the master bedroom.

Placing her bag on the bed, she continued to listen to the fighting next door. This seemed as good a place as any to catch her breath. Sebastian had left three text messages. Biting her lip, she sent a reply. "Safe, no longer with B. Don't worry." She wouldn't risk saying more. Was that the way their life together would be? Half-truths and reassurances that sounded weak even to her ears? Other men? She shrugged.

The acid in her stomach had settled, but she still didn't want to eat. She stretched out on the floor and folded herself into a sitting, forward bend. After holding the position for a minute her cell-phone buzzed. Grabbing it she found a message from Jeremiah. "Tomorrow, two o'clock, Highclere Castle Ceremony." The plan was in motion.

"Do we know his plans?" She typed back, as she pushed her hair out of her face.

"No, just that he expects his men to be in place before the ceremony to hand over King Tut's scarab to the museum."

"Is the bug in his office still in place?"

"We think so, but Bakari is guarded with his words, as if he knows someone is listening."

That paranoia was probably what had kept him alive so long. "Anything else?"

"That's it. All we know is that he plans to take the scarab and it involves a team of his men."

"I'll be there."

"I'll send George to back you up and liaise with MI5. Get some sleep. You'll need it."

"About Sebastian."

"Leave him out of this Sadie."

CHAPTER 41

Sadie had left Bakari's house, but not his heart. Her musky smell lingered in his office, drifting into every crevice of his libido. Taking her on his desk hadn't been the romantic move he'd wanted to make with her, but he couldn't wait any longer. He had grown tired of the man-woman games. He'd wanted her, and now he'd had her.

But once was not enough.

Funny how life always surprises. Chasisi had told him he would only need to be with Sadie once, said one good screw with her would give him a sense of possession, a sense of completion. But it wasn't enough, not nearly enough.

Sadie was the consummate femme-fatale, sensual, sexy and playful. That was the part that flirted with him, but that wasn't the part he'd taken on the desk. He'd made love to the real Sadie, warm, caring and passionate. She may be a spy, but even spies can't act that well. He'd had the real woman.

There was an undeniable attraction between them and now they'd cemented it by making love. Could there be a future for them? If he could stop Chasisi and Gahiji from killing her... He smiled in his empty office. And if the CIA didn't try to cage her spirit, or some weirdoes from her past didn't catch up with her... He started to pick up the items from the top of his desk that now lay strewn all over the floor. And if his family could accept an American woman... He laughed. The impossibility of their relationship just made it all the more tempting, like a taboo just beyond reach.

He'd been seduced by Sadie's charms, taken-in more by her than by any other woman, possibly even more than with Djeserit when he was under her spell.

Sadie. Her soft green eyes came to mind, and her sultry voice calling his name as he moved within her, deep within her. Damn it. He sat back in his chair. She could be his ruin.

He heard a knock on his door. "Come in," he said.

Khalid entered. "I thought you might need me."

Bakari laughed. Yes, everything might work out after all, as long as he stayed in control. "I need you to reach Sadie Stewart in her dreams. Do you know how to do that?"

Khalid smiled.

CHAPTER 42

Sadie fell into a fitful sleep. Her mind drifted back to the scene of horror in the jungles of Nigeria, far from civilization.

The oppressive heat hung in the air, making it hard to breathe. Her hair stuck to her face with sweat. The smell of the wild clung to her nostrils. The sound of wild animals moving behind her in the bush sent tremors up her spine. She was back in the center of it all, feeling helpless and alone—again.

The drums beat loudly with a hard rhythm that would haunt her till her dying breath. Her awareness floated above the scene, unable to stop it. The shaman, dressed in a robe of vibrant oranges and red, bound JaJa to his dead mother's body with thick vines. He danced and chanted to his spirits. The grave digger stood beside him, saying nothing.

Every detail of the nightmare was the same as all the others, until the shaman turned his head and looked directly into Sadie's eyes.

Sadie screamed, but knew no one could hear her. The drums were too loud and help was far away. Why had she strayed away from the others? Why had she thought herself invincible?

This had happened one other time. Her body trembled with fear.

Three black holes tore open on each of the witch doctor's cheeks. Worms slithered from inside his body, crawling through his blood to mount the surface of his eyes. He spat words at Sadie. "Do not think you are safe."

Sadie stared at the transforming figure of the witch doctor. A scream of horror caught in her throat.

"Do not stop Bakari, or the vengeance of the gods will fall upon you and you son."

When Sadie woke in the morning a horrible ache had settled into the center of her forehead. After a long shower she made herself coffee. The feeling that something had happened to her during the night would not leave. It stuck with her, like a bad...nightmare. Was that it?

The ancient Egyptians believed in dream travel. Mitch was convinced that a sorceress had tried to reach her through her dreams before. Had it happened again? Khalid? If so, why didn't she remember it this time? Was he that much more powerful than his mother? What had he done to her in her dream?

Sadie shook her head. Hocus pocus kafooey. Seriously weird stuff. She needed to focus. Today, King Tut's scarab would be revealed.

CHAPTER 43

Sadie planned to arrive at the castle at one thirty, thirty minutes before the event. A rented car waited for her outside the safe house. As she drove through the busy streets of London and into the country, she ran through what she knew about the Carnarvon estate.

A closet *Downton Abbey* fan, she'd picked up some of lore about the castle and its secrets. It stood on a one-thousand-acre estate, which had been the site of a bishop's medieval castle. They'd found evidence of hill forts and habitats dating back to the Iron and Bronze Ages.

At the beginning of the nineteenth century a plain mansion replaced the bishop's castle. It was later extensively renovated in a Jacobethan style by the third earl of Carnarvon. The modern castle was completed in 1878 and called Highclere Castle. It became one of the centers of political and social life of the Victorian era.

But the connection the castle had with ancient Egypt interested her most of all. In the early twentieth century the fifth earl of Carnarvon worked with the famous archaeologist Howard Carter to unearth the tomb of Tutankhamen. He put his fortune into the excavation and took some of the treasures home.

The early Egyptologists thought nothing of bringing back some of their spoils. Most of the Carnarvon Egyptian treasures were later sold to museums to help pay off the family death taxes. But, in the 1970s new Egyptian treasure was found in a cupboard in one of the walls of the castle. Sadie had always wondered if more had been hidden away and forgotten.

Now King Tut's scarab had been found and was about to be shown to the world.

***

Chills ran up Sadie's spine as she drove through the woods and extensive grounds. Sunlight filtered through the morning mist, giving the landscape a mystical sheen. The sheer beauty of the rolling downlands of North Hampshire and the Kennet Valley teleported her mind back to a more pastoral time.

She'd been to the castle once for tea with the countess, had toured the rooms open for the public, and seen the Egyptian exhibit in the cellar. This would be the first time she visited it as a spy.

Ten years ago, when people thought of a castle, they would conjure up a Disney image, or, if they'd traveled their favorite European castle. But today Sadie wagered they'd think of Highclere, its beauty, its majesty, its elegance. *Sure hope Bakari doesn't blow it up.*

She parked in the almost full public lot and sent Jeremiah a text. "Show time."

After a quick visual scan of the area, she got out of the car. Although many people would be dressed up for the occasion, Sadie had chosen to dress down, faded blue jeans, jean jacket and a white blouse. The only jewelry she wore were diamond studs in her ears, a Christmas gift from Sebastian.

With an expensive camera hanging from her neck and a bulging camera bag full of spy gear on her shoulder, she blended well into the scene. She looked like a tourist with money for expensive toys, or possibly a photo-journalist working freelance. After it was all over, Sadie would thank Eleanor for leaving her the gear.

Sadie tied her hair back into a knot at the nape of her neck. She wore her dark glasses and three weapons: a Glock at the base of her spine, her favorite knife strapped to her left leg, just above her boots, and a second gun in her bag.

Three television vans were lined up by the entrance. People with cameras adjusted their lenses and snapped pictures. Their sweat smelled of anticipation. A growing buzz of excitement threaded through the growing crowd. Thirty minutes to go before the hand-over ceremony. She seeded herself into the crowd, avoiding eye contact and headed towards the door.

Three uniformed policemen walked the perimeter of the castle with sniffer dogs. Bakari wouldn't be able to set smoke bombs this time.

A team of four security men monitored the entrance and everyone entering had to go through a screening alcove, the kind that finds weapons. When it was her turn, she zeroed in on the man in command, easy to spot because of the way he firmly held his jaw, part arrogant confidence and part warrior. He looked at her the way all men did and when she smiled back he moved closer.

She leaned towards him, "Is it true the Queen is not expected to attend?" At least the code words weren't about pigeons this time.

Shaking his head, he said, "It is not on her itinerary." His British accent was refined and his aftershave pricey. Had to be MI6. Without blinking he slid a cloaking device into her hand as she put her bag on the table for inspection. "I believe she's busy in London." He stepped back and she walked through the screening doorway without a problem.

The 'saloon', the so called heart of the castle, couldn't possibly hold the number of people who'd turned up. Most of them would remain outside. She'd noticed on her way in that two men were setting up a big screen TV on the side of one of the news vans.

Having so many people left outside had it's up and down side. If something happened inside, she had fewer people to assess and deal with, but if they took the trouble outside they could have reinforcements waiting there, or they could disappear easily into the throng. She noted her exits. Three uniformed security men stood outside, in front of the windows. Another three stood by the arched entrances. Someone had put a lot of money into security.

Walking through the famous arches into the room, she marveled once again at its opulence. Decorated in a Gothic style, there were leather wall coverings that had been in the family since the seventeenth century.

A podium with a microphone had been set up in front of the windows. No sign of the treasure. The furniture had been removed to make room for people and there had to be thirty crammed into the room for the event. *Wonder what the boy king would think of this pomp and ceremony?*

Everything about the event seemed solid. Wait... It was way too normal. She could smell trouble brewing. A shiver stole up her spine. She had to find the abnormality in the scene and she had to find it fast.

To her right four minor British politicians and two Met directors chatted about the museum. She gave them a pass. They were bureaucrats guilty of boring rhetoric, but they weren't thieves. The rest of the crowd could be divided into three groups: regular people, some dressed up for the occasion and others looking as if they'd walked out of a London pub; press people who looked nervous and two people she recognized as belonging to the Egyptian embassy.

Ebony did not appear in the crowd. Nor Chasisi. Who had Bakari sent? Or had he sent anyone?

Maybe her intel was wrong. Maybe he intended to intercept the scarab after it left the castle.

Nah. Her gut told her this was it. Whatever Bakari had planned would happen here and soon. Her chest tightened.

She scanned the faces again, looking for clues. A blond lady in a blue, linen power suit chewed gum. She watched her for a minute. An anomaly. But, nah, she must have just stopped smoking. A tall man scanned the crowd playing with the telephoto lens on his camera. He looked like police, but she was not sure which organization. She studied face after face.

Then she saw them. They weren't together, but they were different. Dressed in dark inconspicuous clothing and looking bored, they speckled the celebrating crowd like pepper. She noticed them because they didn't stand out. No facial tics, no excitement, no awe.

Keeping her eyes on the one standing three yards from her, she pulled her cell-phone from her pocket. She snapped photos of the men and sent them to Jeremiah and to George, her back-up, who must be in place outside by now.

The rising tension in the crowd was palpable. The chatter had risen in tempo and volume. The smell of excitement laced the air. Then everyone hushed. Walking through the middle arches, the eighth earl of Carnarvon and his wife, the countess, appeared, flanked by two security men. The earl had carried a fancy, engraved wooden tray, and on the tray sat a golden box. Out of the corner of her eye, Sadie watched the three men she'd spotted.

Her phone beeped. She checked it. Jeremiah wrote: "Confirmed. Bakari's men. Notified MI6. More back-up on the way. Ten minutes out."

The earl climbed the platform and walked to the center, the countess at his side. He put the box on the podium. "Good evening..." he began.

Bang. A deafening explosion within the house ended his speech.

CHAPTER 44

Chasisi piloted the helicopter. His men stole it from a news agency that morning and they'd been circling the area for the last hour. When his man on the ground cued him that the treasure had been brought into the public view, he lowered the chopper.

Those on the ground paid no attention to him at first, their eyes glued to the TV monitor showing the earl at the podium. But when he came lower a few looked up. One aimed a gun and pulled out a cell-phone. Perhaps, they'd been tipped off.

It didn't stop Chasisi. He carried out his final swoop as planned. His gunman opened the side door, leaned out and fired a missile into the castle. Right on target. The explosion sent shock waves through the air. It unsettled the helicopter, but Chasisi kept control. He thanked his good luck as he rose above the confusion on the ground. Fire, smoke, and at least a hundred frightened people running for their cars.

Gunfire glanced off the side of the chopper, but it didn't take a direct hit. They gained elevation and headed for the drop-off point in a field not far away.

***

Chaos took over. People screamed and pushed their way out of the room. From deeper in the castle, she could hear a different kind of screaming. People had been hurt, and hurt badly. Damn Bakari.

Dark smoke flowed into the room through the open archways burning her eyes and nostrils, impairing her vision. Three men dressed in black moved towards the platform. Her heart raced. She had to get to them.

The shrieking of the security alarms and screams of people filled her ears. No one could hear over it, but the security men should be communicating on their own system. Hopefully, they had a plan. She tried to swallow, but she had little spit left, and what was left had been seasoned with the bitter taste of destruction.

The crowds stampeded out of the room, swearing, and yelling.

Within seconds, she reached the platform, but the scarab was gone. One of the men dressed in black had to have it. But which one? They'd headed in three different directions through the open arches. She swallowed. Her dry throat burned from the toxic crap in the smoke.

Which one had the scarab? What was his destination? It was like playing a shell game on a boardwalk, only the stakes were higher, much higher. Adrenalin pumped through her body, giving her tunnel vision, but that didn't help her make a decision.

Which one? Two moved like trained operatives, agile and athletic. The third was slower. He'd slipped out the doorway. Each carried a satchel over his shoulder. Which one?

Sadie had to guess the thieves' escape route. The sound of the chopper faded quickly, so the assailants weren't likely to be heading to a high point for pick-up. They must be planning to escape on foot, in front of everyone's noses. Bakari had balls of steel. Sweat trickled down her spine. There was only one way to beat a man like that. She needed to be even ballsier.

The security team would monitor, possibly even seal, the exits.

She'd follow the slow guy. Her gut said to go for him, because he was the least likely.

Did he have a limp? If he did, it would be Chasisi for sure; a deadly opponent, but one that needed to be brought down. She pushed her way through the crowds and as soon as she was clear ran in the direction he'd taken. He exchanged his satchel with another man dressed in a conservative business suit then headed through the front door.

A brush pass. Who would the other man be? He headed for the grand staircase. Panting from exertion she climbed the stairs after him, closing the distance between them. As she climbed she pulled out her gun and clicked off the safety. Ten yards, eight, six... one.

At the sound of her safety clicking on, he turned to look at her.

Sadie froze. Bakari stood five steps above her, aiming a gun at her face. "*Habibti*, don't make me do this."

Holding her Glock steady with both hands, she pointed it directly between his eyes. A kill shot. At this distance she couldn't miss. "I can't let you go." Her voice trembled and sounded hoarse. The damn smoke made it hard to breathe.

"This scarab will heal Rashida," he said.

"You hurt people Bakari." *I've been trained to shoot, not to talk. Why the hell am I talking?* She should shoot. Get it over with. Take down her target. Rid the world of a seriously bad-ass guy. But her trigger finger froze. It would not move. It was as if it was... cursed. The sound of African drums beating filled her ears. She shook her head to clear it.

"Give yourself up," she said. If only there was another way... Her whole body trembled. She had to shoot him.

"It's all for Rashida," he said as his eyes darkened to an unfathomable blackness. The click of the safety on his gun echoed in her ears. "You understand. I have no choice—"

A shot rang out. Bakari fell to the ground, holding the cloth bag. The acrid smell of gunpowder flooded the air. Sadie turned to look for the shooter. At the bottom of the stairs stood Sebastian in a shooting stance, arms extended, pointing his Beretta 92 in her direction. Determination was fixed in every muscle of his face, and a killer coldness flattened his eyes, in a way she'd never seen before.

Behind him a figure stepped from the shadows. Khalid Badru. She pointed and Sebastian turned, but the figure had already vanished.

"Freeze," shouted a policeman. Within seconds they were surrounded by uniforms.

***

Sadie breathed a sigh of relief as a middle-aged man with short, brown hair and wispy eyebrows threaded his way through the policemen. She didn't want any of the evidence destroyed. Reginald Kensington, dressed in a beige trench coat and Italian, black leather loafers, was an old buddy of Sadie's from MI5. They'd worked a few missions together, but she didn't know he'd joined this one. He talked into the ear of the head policeman. The man jolted in response to Reggie's words and gave the immediate command for his men, to stand down.

The policeman had just released the handcuffs from Sadie's hands when Reginald made it to her side. "Istanbul?"

His proper English accent flowed over her like a warm shower on a cold morning and she smiled. A tiny glint of light shone in the corner of his hazel eyes.

"The last time I saw you was Istanbul," he said, prompting her again.

"Copenhagen," she replied in code. She was all right. It was over and she could speak freely.

Four policemen were releasing Sebastian. Their expressions clearly indicated that they didn't want to be doing this. One of them sported a black eye. Sebastian had not been easy to restrain.

Reggie touched Sadie's arm and together they approached Bakari's body. The bullet had hit him in the head, throwing his body backwards onto the stairs. Brain matter and blood splayed over several steps. His body lay still.

Sadie's throat constricted. Her chest tightened. She shouldn't feel remorse for the death of a bad-guy, a man so evil that he supplied guns to child warriors and barbarians in the Islamic State. She shouldn't. But she did. When all was said and done, Bakari al-Sharif was a man who loved his family. Love to him meant total commitment. He risked his life, his fortune, and he would say, his karma for his daughter. A man like that had to be admired at least a little. Right?

Okay, so maybe his big cajones and devilish charm had gotten to her.

She gritted her teeth. "Can I see the bag?"

Reginald had been scanning the death scene. His eyes turned to the man beside the satchel and cocked a brow.

"Yes, sir."

Sebastian was suddenly beside her, his large hand caressed the base of her spine.

Reggie opened the bag. "Bloody hell." He turned towards the chief and yelled, "Seal the exits immediately."

"Nothing?" Sadie asked.

"Nothing. We've been duped. King Tut's scarab has been stolen from right under our noses."

CHAPTER 45

Vancouver, Canada
One week later

Chione answered the door of her
Victorian-era Kitsilano house, expecting a neighbour
she'd invited over for morning coffee. Instead, a
young woman dressed in an Express Mail uniform
stood on her door step holding a parcel. "Ms.
DeWolf?"

"Yes." Her senses sharpened.

"Got a parcel. You need to sign for it."

She wasn't expecting anything in the mail,
but she'd known something was heading her way.
That unmistakable feeling of awareness had been
with her since her sister Djeserit died six months
ago.

Taking a deep breath, she wondered if she
could change the future by not accepting her mail.
The air held that distinct, Vancouver autumn smell,
part falling maple and alder leaves and part ocean.

She loved her adopted home. The coastal mountains loomed on the horizon like sentinels.

Years ago she had left Egypt her homeland, for the beauty and serenity of the west coast of Canada, hoping to escape her past and her heritage. But there was no running away from who she was meant to be.

As she grasped the package, a shivery feeling spilled into her hands and slithered up her arms to the base of her skull. "Thank you," she said as she wrote her signature on the tablet.

After the messenger left she took the brown package, the size of a loaf of bread, into her house and placed it on her round table, beside her favorite tarot cards. The creepy awareness that her life was about to turn on its heels remained.

She touched the crystal she wore around her neck and closed her eyes for a moment, then as she lit the candle sitting in the middle of the table, she whispered a prayer of protection. The air in the room stilled.

The package looked so harmless, but she knew it was not. Closing her eyes, she saw images of her younger sister Djeserit. Her gentle smile and wise, gray eyes, deeper than the Nile, called to her. A gift from the grave?

Chione opened her eyes and carefully stripped the paper off the box. Sweat beaded on her forehead and at the nape of her neck. Duct tape had been used to keep the box inside sealed, so she had to fetch scissors to loosen it. With one final rip, the box opened.

Her breath caught. Inside lay Djeserit's ivory wand, nestled in tissue paper. Etched with hieroglyphics   and   charmed   with   ancient incantations it was the most powerful wand she'd ever seen.

Beside the wand lay an envelope with her name typewritten on it. Djeserit would never use a typewriter to craft a note to her. That would be too impersonal. Someone else had sent her this package. Her stomach tingled.

Chione reminded herself to breathe. She had wondered what had happened to Djeserit's wand. No one mentioned it after her death; but then only a few knew how powerful it was. If it fell into the wrong hands... It could give too much power to the dark side.

Tears filled her eyes as she traced the hieroglyphics with her finger tips and memories of her sister flooded her mind. A relic from ancient times, blessed by priests and sorcerers, a talisman of her sister. So many memories. They had practiced together as adepts, but Djeserit had chosen the path of a sorceress, while she turned her back on the arcane knowledge and chose the life of a common woman, albeit in exile.

Djeserit had enjoyed the old ways and had never used her powers to hurt others. She had a kind and loving heart. If only she hadn't fallen in love with Bakari al-Sharif. If only she'd stayed true to the path.

Chione opened the envelope and took out the letter:

Dear Mrs. deWolf,

I wanted to meet you and give Djeserit's wand to you personally, but if you are receiving this letter it means I have died before I could. On your sister's deathbed she begged me to give it to you and to no one else, to entrust its power to your light.

I don't pretend to understand these things, but I want Djeserit's last wishes to be fulfilled.

You must know that she and I have a son, Khalid Badru, who I have just found out about. In an effort to gain his mother's power, he killed her. I do not believe he intended to. She feared he would become an evil sorcerer and tasked me to do what I could to stop him. I am trying to bring him into my family and do what I can, but he must not get this wand. That was Djeserit's greatest fear.

I admired your sister. We were friends for many years. She was my confidant and advisor. I miss her.

Sincerely
Bakari al-Sharif

Tears rolled down Chione's cheeks as she folded the letter. It was all so sad. Had her sister and al-Sharif been born in another time they might have been lovers. Instead they'd each struggled with their feelings and kept them hidden. Now their son was orphaned and out of control. He'd have to be dealt with. She put the letter into the flame of the candle and watched it catch fire. She held it until it singed her finger tips, then she dropped it into onto the table where it burned itself out. The sting of her burns didn't come close to the searing pain in her heart.

Wiping the tears on her cheeks, she resolved to contact the elders in Egypt. They had been her spiritual circle when she practiced magic, and even though years had passed since she talked with them, they would help her. She couldn't keep the wand hidden. Its power would draw people and if it fell into the wrong hands it could be misused.

It would have to be protected and a group could do that better than she could. But the world was changing. Few believed in the old ways—the old magic. Destroying it might be a better option. A quiver of awareness spread across her scalp.

Tonight there would be a full moon. She could do it then.

She heard knocking on her door. It had to be her friend this time. She put the ashes of Bakari's letter into the kitchen sink. "Just a minute," she called out.

The wand couldn't be left in plain sight. She took it out of the box and put it in a hidden drawer in her altar at the side of the room. The lock clicked.

Her friend Hilda was twenty minutes late, but that wasn't unusual. The woman didn't like to run her life by a clock. It would be fun to share a coffee and chat. For a few minutes she would forget the heavy burden she'd just received. She opened the door wide.

But it wasn't her friend standing on her threshold.

A lanky, young man with black hair pulled away from his long angular face stood there. Black stubble shadowed his cocoa- colored skin. The intensity of his dark eyes hit her like a bucket of ice water thrown on her face. She swallowed. It was more his expression than any one physical feature, or even her sixth sense, that told her who he was. "Khalid Badru."

CHAPTER 46

New York,
One week after Bakari's death

"*T*wo men are hunting you.

Be careful." said Mitchell in a text to Sadie. As her plane crossed the Atlantic she tossed the words around in her mind. Why didn't he say more? For that matter, why the hell didn't he phone her?

When she stepped from the elevator on her apartment floor she heard barking. Dashing her plan to drop off her stuff at her place, she headed down the hall to her dog-sitter's door.

As she knocked the puppy's barks grew louder and more urgent. Was that a growl? His small body worked hard to make big-dog sounds.

It took an eternity for the door to open, which made her wonder what Beatrice was up to. Slip, click... slip, click... slip, click. The locks were released and still the door did not open. Sadie reached for the gun in her purse.

The door opened and there stood her neighbor dressed in another pink, jogging suit with a lipstick-stained cigarette dangling from her lips. The puppy launched himself at Sadie's legs. She laughed and reached down to pick him up as she entered the apartment.

Turning around to ask Beatrice how she was doing, Sadie took in a short, burly man in a wife-beater shirt standing behind the open door. He pointed a gun at Sadie's face.

What the hell? His hard eyes, sunk deep into a short forehead, telegraphed a distinct don't-fuck-with-me message. This man had killed before.

"Beatrice?" Sadie asked.

"Look, cheekbones. I don't know what shit you're into, but I don't want to be a part of it. Take your dog and get outta here."

"Shit?"

"That Mitchell guy said you was into dangerous business."

"Oh him. He exaggerates."

"Nah. You can't lie to me. I can read people." She pointed to her head. "There's something about you that just don't add up."

Where should Sadie start? The man hadn't lowered his gun.

"And those two pricks that came by looking for you? Didn't like 'em."

Sadie nodded, trying to understand. Slowly she put the squirmy puppy down on the wooden floor.

The man with the gun walked around her and closed the door.

"Two men were looking for me?" Sadie said.

"Yeah. Strange guys dressed in black. They pushed their way into my apartment and asked a lot of questions. Wanted to know where you were, what you were up to. When I told them about your modeling gig, they just laughed."

"No one asks Beatrice questions." The man had a voice. "Evah."

"I'm sorry," Sadie began.

Beatrice held up her hand to stop her from saying more. "Don't bother wasting your wind. Just get out and stay out."

"I don't know why the men came here."

"Are you as lame a dame as you sound, or is this all part of your act?" Beatrice squinted as if that might help her decide.

Sadie blinked.

"Sheesh." Beatrice waved a hand at her friend to get him to lower his gun.

Casanova ran between them licking and nipping at whatever leg was closest. Sadie bent down to pick him up again and the puppy went wild with slurpy kisses.

"The dog trusts you." Beatrice sounded confused.

The soft, fluffy, chocolate-brown ball of fur, her very own adorable labradoodle puppy, was all over her with his love. Sadie felt herself smile, despite the extraordinary situation she was in. Beatrice walked closer and stroked the pup.

The man snorted. "Are you going to kick her ass out or will I have to do it?"

Beatrice gave Sadie a hard enough look to knock her teeth out. Their eyes connected and held.

Beatrice turned to the guy. "Go take a hike. I'll talk to her alone."

"But—?"

"Do as I say or I'll tell." She didn't say a name. Clearly, she didn't have to. Before she finished her sentence he was up and moving.

"I'll get cigarettes."

"Sit down." Beatrice motioned Sadie to the sofa. "I'll tell you what happened."

With Cassy wiggling in her arms and licking her face with a sandpaper tongue, Sadie sat.

"In the middle of the night Cassy started barking. Never saw him so upset. So I got my revolver and went out to the living room. Two guys with ski masks were goin' through my stuff. Tossing it everywhere." Beatrice walked over to the coffee maker on the kitchen counter and pulled out the carafe.

Sadie nodded, both to the offer of the coffee and to encourage her to tell her more.

Beatrice poured two cups and talked while she walked back to a chair facing Sadie. "I pointed my gun at the first idiot and yelled at him to stop." They both turned and glared at me like I was holding a wader gun or something." She shook her head.

The coffee was bitter, but Sadie took a second sip and smiled.

"Anyway, to make a long story short, after I waved my gun around a few times they told me they were lookin' for you."

"And you told them?"

"Nothin'. I knew nothin'." Beatrice's eyes narrowed.

"Did they leave you alone?"

"I had the gun, remember."

Not many middle-aged women could hold off two thugs. But Beatrice had a steely edge to her, a toughness you just didn't want to play with.

"It was really Cassy that saved me. He warned me so that I could get the jump on them. Good dog, that one."

Sadie stroked his fur. He smelled puppy-fresh. "Did you call the police?"

"Hell no. I don't like them and I'm guessing you don't either."

Sadie had to smile.

"I told the buggers I'd let them go if they told me what they were lookin' for." Beatrice shrugged.

Unbelievable! The woman had bartered with them. They were probably assassins.

"They looked at each other, then back at me. They looked ready to jump me. That's when Vince came in."

"Vince?"

Beatrice tilted her head. "One of my lovers. I thought he was still asleep, but he'd been listening from the bedroom."

Sadie fought her eyebrows to stay down. One of...? How many men did Beatrice have?

"Anyway Vince... he's a rough one, ya know."

"Is he the guy you just sent out?"

"Nah, that one works for him. My Vincent is seriously, a switch blade carrying guy from the shadows. No one crosses him and lives. And he don't like people messing with me neither."

Sadie's eyebrows shot up. She couldn't hold them down any longer.

"The two guys froze when they saw him probably wet their pants. Vince says to me, 'You want me to have my men work on them, honey?'"

Now Sadie smiled.

"Nah, I said. I think they're ready to talk. And they did. Slowly at first, but then Vince got out his blade. They told us you have a map and they want it or they'll have to kill you. I got the feeling they wanted to do both."

"A map?"

"That's what they said. Vince wanted to rough them up to make sure they didn't return, but I wouldn't let him. I don't want no blood in my home. They left."

"So that other man is protecting you?"

"Yeah Vince insisted he be here, at least until you returned. Now I'll send him home unless you want him."

"Uh, no thanks." Sadie laughed. "Beatrice, you are one hell of a dog-sitter. I don't know how to thank you."

Beatrice lifted her hand to stop Sadie from saying more. "Hey, I liked the excitement. Being old can get boring."

Sadie took another sip of the coffee. "I was in London on a shoot," she began and proceeded to tell her a long story that had actually happened to her a month ago, complete with ego-centric models, cocaine orgies and a drunken photographer who had a fetish for stilettos. Beatrice nodded politely, but avoided eye contact. When she felt it was time to go, Sadie stood and made her excuses.

Beatrice helped her down the hallway with all the dog stuff. Cassy followed them leaping at their legs.

When they were in Sadie's apartment, Sadie reached into her purse for money. Beatrice shook her head. "I like your dog, Sadie. I don't want your money."

"Look, I'm sorry for all your trouble. I really appreciate your help." She searched for the right words. "Maybe you would do it again sometime?" There would be no better person to take care of Casanova.

"Sure. But don't bother bullshitting me again." With that Beatrice opened the door and left.

Sadie laughed.

***

Later that night she connected with Mitchell by phone.

"What the hell, Mitch?"

"I'm in Singapore on a shoot," he said. "I didn't want to say more on my cell. I didn't think it would be safe."

And so they talked about Beatrice, the weather and fashion and model gossip. The sound of his familiar voice comforted her, almost as much as Cassy's wet nose on her neck. It felt good to be home.

But there were still loose ends… and a map.

CHAPTER 47

Langley
The next day

Sadie's stilettos clicked as she walked down the long hallway to Jeremiah's office. Fighting against her usual hate-the-stuffy-office reactions, she held her chin high, greeting everyone she passed with a smile.

Jeremiah nodded as she entered and finished his phone conversation with, "Later."

Sitting in the leather office chair opposite his desk, she scanned the room for changes, but there were none. The same three computer screens spanned his desk. He wore a boring business suit with an open collared white shirt. His chess set, the one she'd thrown in the garbage six moths ago, sat to the left of his keyboard. "Good morning, Jeremiah."

A slow, thin-lipped smile spread across his perfectly shaved face. "Mornin' sugar."

"Got my report?"

His amber eyes blazed with a fiery energy. He didn't have time for small talk. She shifted her butt in the chair, which seemed more uncomfortable than she remembered. "For the record, I did try to save the scarab."

Jeremiah chuckled. "The Brits have their knickers in a knot."

"It's all in my report. I followed my gut and I was wrong."

"You brought down one of the most dangerous men in the world. How wrong is that?"

"Sebastian pulled the trigger."

"Because of you. You have a way of getting men to do things for you." His tone wasn't lewd, just matter of fact.

"Friggin' hell." The light bulb in her head turned on. "My real mission was to eliminate Bakari al-Sharif, not to bring you back a relic."

A slow, cynical smile crossed his wizened face. "Sadie, there are many kinds of treasure in this world. The scarab will resurface sometime, I'm sure. But the great Anubis will not. I call that a victory."

She took a deep breath. "He wasn't all bad, you know."

"No one is all-anything, Sadie. But falling for the slime on a snake is not wise."

She groaned. "Why didn't you just tell me to take him out? I had lots of opportunity. Why did you play me, as well as him?"

Jeremiah leaned back in his chair. "The higher-ups wanted both the scarab and the man. I'm happy to get the man."

"You could have used an assassin."

"Could have. But his security team had already killed two of our best. You, sugar, were the only operative who could get close enough."

"You know from my psych profile that I'm not a hit woman."

"Honey, you got the job done. In this business, that's all that matters."

The razor sharp edge of his logic could be really annoying. Part of her, the non-emotional part, had to admit he was right. But her heart felt used, like a dirty old dish rag. She chewed her bottom lip.

"Did you sleep with him?"

She winked at Jeremiah. "That's on a need to know basis." Although he must have heard the audio-tape.

He gave a strangled laugh and looked away. "Let me update you. Last night, Chasisi al-Sharif was found dead in his bedroom at the family's Cairo estate. The official cause of death—snake bite. That leaves only one brother, Hasam, to run the family arms business, and in my opinion he can't do it alone. Someone will take him out."

"Did we kill him?"

"Not to my knowledge. Also, the scarab hasn't surfaced. Rashida is dying. The doctors give her a week to live."

Snake bite? "Do you have any idea who—"

"None, though I suspect Khalid wanted no opposition to his inheritance. To be honest, I don't care. One less arms dealer. His empire in ruins. It's all good."

"Eboni?"

Jeremiah shrugged.

She leaned back in her chair. Bakari and Chasisi dead. That was a lot to take in. "Have you any more information on the KOTL?"

"Unfortunately not. Keep your eyes open, sugar. Someone wants you dead."

What else was new? She pushed a long curly tendril of hair away from her face. She could tell him about the men after the map. Nah, she'd leave that for later. "What now?" she said.

"It's time for you to make a decision," he said.

She knew what he meant. Did she want to be a spook again? "Only on my terms."

He chuckled. "Which are?"

"I don't want you to hold back information again."

His gaze drifted to the ceiling. "You can't ask for the impossible."

"I get it. There's a reason for the need-to-know policy around here, but it's stifling at best and outright dangerous at worst. If I'm to sign up again, I want to know all aspects of any mission, before you send me in. None of this risking my life, blind folded. I don't think that's asking too much."

His eyes remained on the ceiling as if an enigmatic message slid along the white paint. "Sometimes I don't even have all the facts."

Silence settled in the room slow and steady like an avalanche of sand. The smell of his Earl Grey tea reached her senses. She wanted back in the fold, but she had to get him to understand her position.

Scrunching his mouth as if the milk in his tea had suddenly soured, he sat up and gave her his interrogator's look again. "I have two choices here. Only two. I can lie to you and say I'll tell you everything I know at all times. If I didn't get fired for doing that, I'd be given little information. Or…"

"Or?"

"You can trust me to tell you as much as I can."

"Trust?" A master spy? She laughed.

"You know that I have your best interest—"

"Bull shit. You'll always put the mission first. So don't even try to tell me that you care about me."

A cloud of hurt crossed his eyes for a second before he hardened them. "I do care."

Shit. More silence.

"I could have gotten killed when you sent me after Bakari the first time, with only half a deck of cards. You could have told me more." She fought the tears of anger that the memory brought back to her.

He steepled his hands on his desk. "I've already apologized for that. It was a bad call, but one that wasn't mine."

She'd figured as much. "So why should I trust you, or them." She waved her hand in the air to include the whole building.

"Sadie." His eyes softened like a con man's.

Her back firmed. "Don't sweet talk me. Your southern charm won't cut it this time."

He smiled. "I can only promise to do my best. You know me well enough to know that I will do that."

"I'll walk if it happens again."

"Understood."

She rose to leave the room, ready to sign the endless forms in the stuffy office down the hall, but his voice stopped her.

"Now, I have one condition."

One? "Shoot."

"Get rid of the Dutch guy."

She leaned over his desk. "Fuck you."

"Sadie, sit down and listen to me."

"I'll stand, thank you." She crossed her arms in front of her.

"Sebastian Wilde is dangerous."

"But..."

He put his hand up to stop her from saying more. "Hear me out. The man is a wild card. He keeps turning up at the worst times. I know he saved your life this time, but the two of you might not be so lucky the next time. Sooner or later, his interest in you will interfere with your mission and put you both in danger."

"I love him."

Jeremiah sighed. "Go meet him in Venice, then, just as you planned. Spend time together. Let yourself enjoy being in love. Then end it." He shook his head as she opened her mouth to speak. "You know it's the best thing for both of you."

Her knees trembled. The last thing she wanted was to put Sebastian in danger. She'd find a way to keep him away from her work. "Jeremiah..."

As if he read her thoughts, he shook his head. "Spies fall in love with civilians, but they don't stay in love."

CHAPTER 48

Back in Venice
Two weeks later

*S*adie leaned her back against the hull of the yacht as Sebastian steered them down the Grand Canal. Sated from a week of the best sex— ever—she'd run out of words. She looked out at the canal. How lucky could she be?

The morning light reflected off the water, accentuating its unique aqua color, a Caribbean blue interwoven with dark-navy tendrils of waves from the north. It teamed with energy. The sun danced on the top of the waves like magic. The breeze off the Adriatic Sea blew through her hair. She inhaled deeply. Could life get any better?

The gondolas moored at the sides of the canals waited for the day to truly begin, to take lovers under the Bridge of Sighs, past historic castles, three centuries old. Venice was a city of secrets and mystery, but it was also a place of love.

A *vaporetto* chugged past them filled with commuters and tourists. A woman holding a baby in her arms smiled at Sadie, the smile of contentment, of knowing who you are and what you are meant to do. That's exactly how Sadie felt. Everything in her life had happened for a reason, and it all led to this moment. She felt more truly herself than ever before. She was both a spy and a woman. The two parts of her were woven too tightly together to be pulled apart. She would live a double life as long as she lived.

In one hour, her train would leave for Paris. It was time to end things with Sebastian. She let that thought wash over her.

During their time together she'd stolen moments to think about their relationship, but then he'd kiss her, or tickle her, or... jump her. It was impossible to think about breaking up with Sebastian when she lay by his side. But she couldn't send him a Dear John letter either. He deserved better.

Their attraction wasn't just physical. Though he was an amazing lover. Memories of her second wish, which he granted two hours ago, lingered in her mind. She could still feel his strong arms holding her close, whispering in her ear, "I love you."

No it wasn't all physical. Never had she met such a wonderful man, honest, trusting, caring and fun-loving. He looked tough, but he had a big heart and he had opened it wide to her, only to her. He'd do anything for her. He had killed for her. What more could she want?

Safety. Safety for herself and for him.

The world of espionage called her. She loved the excitement, the thrill of the chase, and knowing that she could make a difference in this fucked-up world. That knowledge ran in her blood. She had to continue working for the CIA. Her skills were needed. It sounded cheesy when she said it out loud, but in her heart she knew it to be the truth. The world could so easily fall into barbarism. She would do whatever she could to prevent that.

Jeremiah's words echoed in her ears. "Spies don't stay in love." Her gut wrenched.

Sebastian steered the boat into the docking area of the train station. He threw the bow-line to a man standing on the dock. He turned to look at her, but she couldn't meet his eyes. She didn't want him to see that there were tears in hers. He jumped onto the dock. She scrambled up without help and stood beside him.

They walked towards the station together. Sebastian rolled her luggage. It made a whirring sound as it rolled on the hard surface. They didn't speak. During the whole week they'd avoided speaking about their relationship. She'd asked him to use condoms and they didn't discuss why. They'd both said the love word many times, but neither had mentioned the future. Now it was time to part. They had to say something about their future.

But how could she? Could she tell him how much she loved him and how much she would miss him? Maybe love was more a curse than a blessing after all.

They walked side by side. Inside the station they checked the schedule. The train was still running on time. A good thing. They stood their looking at the large wall of information as if it held some secret message. She swallowed. "Sebastian?"

He took her hands in his and pulled her close. Resting his forehead on hers, he spoke softly. "I love you, Sadie."

"I'm a spook."

"I know." Sadness laced his tense voice.

"I can't give up my double life. Not even for you." A tear spilled from her eye.

"Maybe not now, but..."

"Sebastian, I know myself. I will always be a spy."

"And I will always love you."

Her tears fell freely now. "I don't want us to end." Where did the words come from? She didn't mean to say them. They spilled out.

He let go of her hand and wiped the tears from her cheeks with tender fingers. His blue than blue eyes caressed hers. "*Mijn liefje*, you will never lose me."

"But we can't continue like this." The thought of endless goodbyes in train stations around the world felt wrong.

"I agree."

Her gut wrenched. This felt all wrong.

"I want you to move in with me."

"Are you out of your mind?"

He laughed. "Possibly, but it's the best idea I can come up with."

"In Amsterdam?" The image of his well-appointed flat on the top of a canal house on the Herengracht came to mind, cozy, convenient and seductive.

"When you're working in Europe, my place in Amsterdam can be our base. I have my friend Seamus upgrading the security system right now. I asked him to make it fit for the queen of spies." Seamus McPherson worked at Interpol and would do a good job. "When you're working in the states, I figured your apartment in New York could be our base. As long as we don't put my cat with your dog, we can make this work."

For one glorious moment she thought they could, but then all her fears rushed back. "Sebastian, I can't put you in danger."

"I don't mind being in danger, as long as I get to be with you." His fingers traced the side of her cheek. "And yes, I do like puppies."

His love echoed through every cell of her body. How could she refuse? "It won't be easy."

"Nothing about you is easy. All I ask is that you're straight with me. Tell me where you are. Don't hold back."

Right. Spies have secrets. She'd never be able to tell him everything, but then, what sane woman tells her man everything? She'd just have a few more secrets than the average woman. "I can only promise to try."

He reached into the pocket of his jacket and brought out a small white velvet jewelry box tied with a blue satin ribbon. "The night the assassin tried to kill you I'd planned to ask you to live with me. And if you said yes, I planned to give you this present to commemorate our new beginning."

A new beginning. Is that what they needed? She pulled on the ribbon and opened the lid. A beautiful sapphire and diamond bracelet lay inside.

She sighed. How could she make this work? Looking into his eyes, she said, "It's gorgeous." She opened the catch and put it around her wrist. The gems glistened in the morning light. Her heart danced. Such a perfect gift. She touched his face. "I love you with all my heart, Sebastian—"

He put a finger to her mouth to stop her saying more. "I love you, Sadie."

His words echoed through her body. Her shoulders relaxed. What was the point in fighting her feelings? She touched his chest wanting to get closer to him. Quirking a brow, she asked, "Does this mean I get my third wish?"

That heated look returned to his pale blue eyes, the one that put her libido on extra high. His full, sensual lips turned into his killer smile, making her knees wobbly. He leaned closer and, in a low, husky voice, said, "Want to tell it to me again."

Her body rippled with expectation. Oh my, yes. Yes. Yes. Yes. "The two of us, alone..."

He kissed her neck in her sweet spot and she lost her words.

"I need details," he said. "Lots and lots of details." He kissed her again this time on her mouth.

She did like details. Could she have two lives, and one true love? Sadie would find a way.

Her life was complicated.

∞

The End

Dear Readers,

Welcome to the world of the modern Mata Hari. If you enjoyed reading Sadie's story, please help me spread the word about the series. Consider telling your friends about the book and writing a review (on Amazon, Goodreads, etc.). Just a few words will make a huge difference in my writing world. Word of mouth and written reviews are pure gold for budding writers.

My website is my home on the Internet http://www.jo-anncarson.com. There you can find links to my newsletter, blog, Facebook Twitter and Pinterest.

To send me a personal note, email me at connect@jo-anncarson.com. I'd love to hear your thoughts on the story.

On the next page you'll find information about the other books in the Mata Hari Series.

Thank you for reading my story.

Best Wish
Jo-Ann Carson

Acknowledgements

Ancient Danger took over a year to write and publish. I couldn't have done it without the support of a wonderful group of people. In particular I'd like to acknowledge:

My husband, Piet, who patiently listened to every wild idea I came up with and encouraged me to "go for it."

Rosalind Villers for giving Sadie's labradoodle puppy his name: Casanova.

Dr. Philip Newey, my copy-editor, who straightened out my grammar.

Nina French, my cover designer extraordinaire.

Angela Sanders, a fellow writer, who shared with me her expertise about perfume.

And last, but never least, my writing buddies who support and inspire me.

All errors are my own.

The Mata Hari Series

Let me tell you about the other stories in the series.

Covert Danger
A single woman — A double life

High fashion model, Sadie Stewart, is a dedicated undercover CIA agent used to getting her man. But this time she's chasing a power-hungry international arms dealer stealing ancient Egyptian amulets. Brilliant, ruthless and slightly wacko, he's a hard catch. She's willing to risk everything to stop him, but the handsome Sebastian Wilde, who looks like a modern Viking, keeps getting in her way. Her independence is shaken as he stirs feelings in her that she thought only existed in fairy tales. Can she put their attraction aside and get the job done?

When Sebastian sees Sadie in a high-speed motor-boat flying down the Grand Canal in Venice, with the Italian military police hot on her tail, her beauty and courage intrigue him. He has a personal vendetta to stop the trading of looted art, and when it looks as though she's involved in that shady world, he decides to stop her. Could the femme fatale really be that evil?

Their adventure spans the globe, with scenes in Venice, Florence, Amsterdam, Cairo and New York.

Can they work together and stop the heist planned for the Met Museum of Art? Protecting the relics becomes their shared goal, but it's not all about ancient magic and power. Love hangs in the balance.

Available from Amazon.

Born of Magic

The Egyptian sorceress wants a child of her own. The arms-dealer wants power at any cost. Their desires conceive a son destined to change the world.

Available from Amazon

Coming Soon:

Eternal Danger,#4
Till Danger Do Us Part, #5

About the Author

Jo-Ann Carson has lived most of her life on islands off the west coast of Canada, surrounded by snow covered mountains, lush rain forests and pristine beaches.

Growing up, she dreamed of traveling the world like James Bond, finding archeological treasures like Indiana Jones, and finding true love. In her Mata Hari Series she combines elements of adventure, danger and steamy romance.